glitter GiRL

DISCARD

toni runkle and **stephen webb**

sourcebooks
jabberwocky

Sourcebooks and the colophon are registered trademarks of Sourcebooks, Inc.

The characters and events portrayed in this book are fictitious or are used fictitiously. Any similarity to real persons, living or dead, is purely coincidental and not intended by the author.

Published by Sourcebooks Jabberwocky, an imprint of Sourcebooks, Inc.
P.O. Box 4410, Naperville, Illinois 60567-4410
(630) 961-3900
Fax: (630) 961-2168
www.jabberwockykids.com

Library of Congress Cataloging-in-Publication data is on file with the publisher.

Source of Production: Versa Press, East Peoria, Illinois, USA
Date of Production: October 2013
Run Number: 21586

Printed and bound in the United States of America.
VP 10 9 8 7 6 5 4 3 2 1

For Katrina and Julia, our daughters,
our inspiration, our joy.

Chapter 1

All That Glitters Comes via UPS

There it was. In the middle of the Connors's living room. The Box. It had been shipped overnight from Los Angeles. Kat had to look at it twice before the reality sank in. It was her name all right: Ms. Katherine Connors, 5473 Jasmine Court, Carmel, Indiana. Her name looked funny there on the box, even though she'd seen it a million times before on papers, report cards, and the Christmas cards that she and her BFF Jules always sent to each other.

But this box was special.

This box was going to make her the first Glitter Girl in all of Indiana.

Maybe no one had heard of Glitter Girl yet, but that was about to change, and Kat was *how* that was going to happen.

Glitter Girl was a new line of products for teens and tweens. Kat hated that word, "tween." *Who invented it?* she wondered. This company in California (Remoulet Worldwide, Inc., according to Kat's googling on the matter) was going to start selling these products next month.

But before that, Remoulet Worldwide, Inc. wanted to get *everybody* excited about it.

That's where Kat Connors came in. And that's why the box ended up in the middle of her living room. Inside that box was simply *every* Glitter Girl product that any girl could ever want. Kat's hand reached closer to the box; she could only imagine what treasures were waiting inside.

"No, Kat," she told herself, pulling her hand back. "You promised Mom you wouldn't touch the box until the sleepover tonight when Jules and everyone else is here."

Kat told herself that, but it's hard to listen to yourself sometimes, especially with all that *stuff* sitting right in front of you. Lip gloss! In who knows how many different shades! And every cool other thing in the history of coolness! And they were giving it all to Kat. For free!

As her hand still hovered over the box, Kat thought about how and why this package came to her in the first place. And how she knew, just *knew,* that this box would change her life. Forever. Obviously, this was no ordinary box. Which made sense. Because Kat Connors was no ordinary girl. She was an Alpha Girl.

Chapter 2

As Chelsea Ambrose, Jr. VP, Likes It

The new mint-green convertible shimmered in the LA sun as it pulled into the parking lot at Remoulet Worldwide, Inc. A perfectly pedicured toe peeked out of its open-toed sandal and stepped down on the gas pedal. The convertible found its way to a spot with a name on it: "Chelsea Ambrose, Junior Vice President." That same Chelsea Ambrose took a deep breath before getting out of the car.

Today was the day that she was going to "wow" them. She was going to present her new marketing plan for Glitter Girl to the Remoulet board of directors. Glitter Girl was a new line of makeup, accessories, and style products aimed at the teen and tween market. (Chelsea loved that word, "tween." *Who invented it?*) The board of directors at the company included a grand total of zero women, which was just fine with Chelsea. She was hired to bring a woman's touch to the marketing department, and bring it she would.

Chelsea's heels clicked as she crossed the lobby and got into the elevator alone. She adjusted the lapel of her jacket and checked her lipstick and makeup in the reflection of the elevator door. Perfect. Her smarts, ambition, and supermodel looks had gotten her this far; it wouldn't take much more to carry her over the finish line. She pressed "35" on the elevator button and started to ascend to the top floor—where all the big decisions got made, the place where she hoped to have a corner office very soon.

As Chelsea opened the door to the boardroom, she saw ten suits around the table.

"Gentlemen, good morning," Chelsea said, giving them her best homecoming queen smile. "I know you're busy men, so I'll keep my presentation brief."

"This better be good," one of the suits said, already putting a tiny hole in Chelsea's confidence balloon. She recognized him as Gregory Remoulet, the CEO of the entire company. She'd walked by the huge painting of him in the lobby a thousand times. Still in shape and handsome at fifty-six, he was the son of the company founder and, from all the gossip around the water cooler, not a man to be trifled with.

Undaunted, Chelsea nodded to an assistant, who dimmed the lights. Chelsea clicked her laptop a few times, and PowerPoint presentation slides lit up the room as she began her sales pitch.

"How have companies launched products in the past?" she said, circling the room like a lioness moving in on a herd of defenseless gazelles. "They've spent millions of dollars on print ads, run commercials at the Super Bowl, and basically pummeled their brand into the consciousness of potential customers with blunt instruments. It was effective, but very expensive."

"You're not kidding," one of the nameless suits said. "Those Jessica Aguirre infomercials have cost us a bundle." He was referring to the ad campaign for Remoulet's signature product, CleanSweep, a facial cream that absolutely *positively* removed all traces of acne from the teenage face. They had signed an exclusive contract with teen singer Jessica Aguirre to be the face of the campaign and had flooded the airwaves with infomercials and ads that were played constantly.

"It was a great campaign for its day. Mr. Remoulet, you and your team really put the company on the map in personal-care products," Chelsea continued. "However, times have changed. Forget TV ads. These are the days of Facebook, YouTube, and Twitter, where one day you're singing a song in your jammies in your living room and the next you're selling out stadiums.

"This is what kids are into today. They don't want

adults or even a celebrity to tell them what to buy. They look to their friends and classmates to confirm their style choices. To sell Glitter Girl, I propose we harness this, the teenage girl's most primal need—the need for the approval of her peers—and combine it with the power of twenty-first-century technology."

"And how exactly do we do that?" asked Remoulet, clearly intrigued.

"With something so innocent that nobody would expect it. We infiltrate the teenage slumber party! What could be more wholesome? These rites of passage have been going on forever, but no one has seen their potential as profit-generating mechanisms until now. We start by picking fifty girls to host fifty slumber parties on the same night, one in each state in the nation. We make sure everyone at the party is draped in Glitter Girl products, and by the time each girl gets back home to her computer the next morning, our campaign will be well on its way."

"So that's it? A slumber party?" said one executive, clearly not yet on board.

"The parties are just the start," replied Chelsea. "At the same time, we pit these fifty girls *against* each other by manufacturing the biggest popularity contest this country's ever seen! And at the end of it, we select one of them as the new

Face of Glitter Girl. We design our print and broadcast campaign around her, this girl that we've plucked out of obscurity, and we announce it all on our website. They'll be falling over themselves to move our products. Before you know it, Glitter Girl will be on the lips of every girl in the country, and at a fraction of the cost of a huge marketing campaign."

"But how are you going to choose these girls?" said Remoulet, looking over the figures in front of him in his marketing packet.

Chelsea smiled. "It's already been taken care of. If you look in the back of your marketing packet, you'll see names and bios of each of the fifty girls. We call them our 'Alpha Girls.'"

"Alpha what?" said one of the suits.

"Alpha Girls," Chelsea said, as she clicked her laptop again and a slideshow of the fifty girls began on the screen behind her. "Alpha is the first letter of the Greek alphabet, and these are the first girls that other girls look to for guidance. Guidance on fashion, music…well, almost anything that matters to girls at this age. They're the most popular girls in school times ten! They are the trendsetters. They've got blogs with a nation of readers, Twitter feeds with thousands of followers, and they wield enormous influence over the girls in their community.

"Take this girl Kat Connors from Indiana," said Chelsea, stopping the slide show on a close-up photo of Kat. "She keeps a style blog, and we've been secretly tracking her picks for six months. She's been ahead of the curve on almost every trend, including the unexpected resurgence of tartan plaid last April. Kat and these other girls are media-savvy instruments waiting to be played. We know from our research that once we get an Alpha Girl to start wearing and using our products, the rest of the pack, if you will, will follow along."

"You make them sound like a bunch of animals," said Remoulet.

"Not animals," Chelsea said, "something far more dangerous when provoked—teenagers."

"But how do you know this Connors girl and the other Alphas will even like our products?"

"Oh, trust me, there's no way they won't," said Chelsea smiling slyly. "I'll see to it."

"It all seems, I don't know, a little underhanded," said Remoulet, looking at Kat's picture. "I like it!"

Chelsea wasn't quite sure how long the discussion among the executives lasted or even what was said. It was all a magnificent blur when she thought about it later, like how some brides describe their wedding day. But she did know they bought her plan hook, eyeliner, and proverbial sinker.

"It's settled then," said Chelsea, packing up her laptop, "I'll go to Indiana to personally supervise the Connors girl, and we'll dispatch reps to each of the other states. We should have hard numbers within a week of the slumber parties."

She noted, with great satisfaction, the jealous looks she saw around the table. The idea had been so simple and so awful that the other executives must have been surprised that their own devious brains hadn't cooked it up. But how could they have? They were men. They didn't know about girls and how they wanted—not wanted—*ached* to fit in. But Chelsea knew and she figured out how to turn that ache into cold, hard cash. "Alpha Girls," as Chelsea had called them, were the key. And Chelsea knew full well that it was Alpha Girls who ran the world.

And how did Chelsea know these Alpha Girls so well?

It takes one to know one.

Chapter 3

The Merry Maids of Wendell Willkie Junior High

"Did you even *know* what that geometry homework was about?" laughed eighth grader Kat Connors as she headed into Wendell Willkie Junior High. "I mean, really? Who was Pythagoras? And why is he bothering us with his silly theorem?"

"It has to do with triangles," said Jules Finch, Kat's BFF and neighbor since they were two years old. Jules was busy wrangling her clunky math textbook out of her backpack.

Kat, whose math textbook was nowhere to be seen, was dressed head to toe in the trendiest outfit ever and looking quite fabulous, thank you very much, as she found her way to her locker right outside Mr. Adams's science lab.

"Hey, girl!" she yelled to Candace Mack, a pint-sized seventh grader moving in the other direction. "Rockin' the high pony today! Looking totally therocious!"

"Therocious" was Kat's word. She made it up last year and it meant thoroughly ferocious—in other words, the coolest thing possible.

"Thanks, Kat!" replied the beaming Candace as she scampered to catch up to her admiring friends, who were impressed she'd been spoken to by "the" Kat Connors.

Jules looked at Kat. "You sure made her day. That was really nice of you."

"Well, I remember when we were that age. The upper-grade kids were so nasty to us. I hated it."

"Nice to see you're using your 'immense influence' in positive ways," laughed Jules.

"Well, like all those who wield power, I must always use it for good and never for evil. I'm kinda like Spider-Man or the Justice League or something."

"Oh yeah, right. You're *exactly* like Spider-Man," said Jules, closing her locker door. "I was just thinking that myself."

"Shut up," laughed Kat. "You know what I mean."

Even though the first bell had already rung, Kat was clearly not in a hurry to get to class. Instead, she lingered by the lockers. It was here she could always be found between classes and before and after school, surrounded by admiring girls and the occasional boy who was brave enough to approach Kat and make an attempt at small talk or being clever.

"Anyway, back to that triangle thingy," said Kat as she deftly maneuvered her own hair into a fishtail braid. "Jules, we totally have to have a study party on this one after school. You bring the brains and I'll supply the popcorn."

"It's actually pretty simple. I'll explain it to you after you're finished holding court," said the more studious Jules.

That's what Jules called this daily routine anyway—"holding court." Jules, who was way into the Renaissance and was vice president of the school's Shakespeare Club, had told Kat that was what royalty used to do. They'd have people come to court and pay homage to them.

Kat wasn't sure if it was a compliment or if Jules was being sarcastic. It was hard to tell with Jules lately. She sure didn't seem too keen on Kat's newfound popularity since they'd hit junior high last year. But Kat couldn't help it if the other girls gravitated toward her and looked to her for what was "in" and "cool." It wasn't like she set out to do it. Her mom, Trudy, said it was "in her blood." The Connors women, they of honey blond hair, fair skin, and striking blue eyes, were always ahead of the curve on just about everything. They just *knew* what was what.

• • •

"Kat! Kat! Check it out! I got it!" the girls heard over the morning buzz in the hallways. It was Zoe Palmer, one of Kat's new "junior high" BFFs. Her long, black, perfectly straightened hair sailed behind her as she pushed her way through the crowded hallway. Tagging along behind her, struggling to keep up, was Darcy Riddle, Zoe's redheaded constant companion.

The two girls dodged the hordes and arrived breathless at Kat's side. In Zoe's expertly manicured hand was something white and sleek. "My parents finally caved and got me the new iPhone!"

"That's great, Zoe," said Kat genuinely. "Make sure you watch your data usage, though. The first time my dad saw *my* phone bill, he totally freaked out."

Zoe held the phone as if it were a precious gem. "I love it. It's just so cool! And it's just like yours, Kat. I'm so glad I finally 'convinced' my parents to buy it." She made little air quotes with her fingers on the word "convinced."

"Wow. I guess whining *is* an effective negotiating tool," snarked Jules. She had finished wrestling the books out of her backpack and was now leaning against a windowsill reading a tattered paperback copy of Shakespeare's poems.

Kat cringed. *Uh-oh. Here we go again*, she thought.

Kat watched as Zoe shot Jules a hostile look. Zoe clearly didn't like Jules who, with her shaggy brown hair, "Save the Whales" T-shirt, camouflage pants, and black Converse (who wears *those* anymore?) clearly *did not* fit in with Kat's new besties.

"For your information, I didn't whine. I looked around on the Internet for articles on missing children and left them up on my laptop screen where I knew my mom would see them," Zoe shot back proudly.

"You *scared* your mom into getting you a new phone? Wow. What a proud moment," said Jules, more than a little disgusted.

"Yeah. I wish I had thought of it. The plan was an absolute perspiration!" offered Darcy, her red curls bouncing in excitement.

"I think you mean 'inspiration,' Darce," said Kat, trying to be helpful.

"I do?" asked Darcy, not quite sure what she had said that was wrong.

Before Jules could open her mouth to say something that would undoubtedly create more tension in the group, Kat jumped in. "Well, I think it's great you got the phone, Zoe, and I think we can *all* agree that it's important to stay in contact with our parents."

Before they could or couldn't agree, the second bell rang.

"Gotta go, peeps," said Zoe. "Mrs. Jolly wants me to come by her room and explain why I'm dropping out of choir this year."

"Why *are* you? I thought your dream was to be a pop star," Kat asked.

"Exactly. Stars aren't part of a choir," sniffed Zoe. "They're *backed* by a choir. If I want to be a star, gotta start thinking like one. Later, ladies!"

Zoe sashayed down the corridor, deliberately causing her lustrous hair to swish from side to side.

"See you guys tomorrow." Darcy smiled, heading toward the exit.

"Uh, Darce. It's first period," said Kat.

"Oh yeah, right. Silly me," giggled Darcy. She looked around puzzled for a moment, trying to get her bearings. Finally, the lightbulb went on, her face lit up, and she headed down the hall to her class.

Kat shook her head and then looked accusingly over at Jules. "How can someone who is so committed to humanity and saving the world—and peace, love, and understanding—be so judgmental?"

"Sorry. It's the smell of all those hair products. Makes me a little nuts," replied Jules, faking a spastic attack.

Kat laughed. Even though Jules didn't quite fit in with her new friends, or even junior high school in general, she was still the smartest, funniest person Kat knew and could always make her laugh.

As they headed into science class, they were stopped by Ms. Donovan, the frumpy, bespectacled teacher who ran the school's Shakespeare Club. Though she was barely thirty, she dressed more like someone's grandma than the young woman she supposedly was.

"Lady Jules. Pray thee. Hast thou come up with any ideas for thy sonnet?" asked Ms. Donovan in a fake English accent that was more fake than it was English.

"Not yet, Mistress Donovan. Sure 'tis a burden to choose just the right poem. But I'm working on it," answered Jules in an actually quite spot-on English accent.

"Well, let me know if you need any help. I am quite the expert, you know," continued Ms. Donovan sounding less British as she went.

"Have you ever considered getting contacts, Ms. Donovan?" asked Kat. She had been scrutinizing the nerdish teacher's appearance like the host of one of those extreme makeover shows you see all over cable.

Ms. Donovan looked over to Kat as if noticing her for the first time but in reality was deliberately ignoring her.

"Because, you know, they would really help show off your face," continued Kat.

Ms. Donovan was not particularly fond of Kat or her type (meaning popular girls, not ever having been one herself). "True beauty comes from within, Ms. Connors. Not from superficial trappings," she sniffed as she self-consciously straightened her glasses and walked away.

Kat shook her head. "Too bad. If Ms. Donovan externalized some of that inner beauty and added a superficial trapping or two, she might score a date with the hot new basketball coach over there. I hear he's single."

Jules looked over at the tall, buffed-out and impossibly handsome Coach Scofield, who at first glance appeared to be looking at trophies in a glass display case. But as he smoothed back his hair, Jules realized he was actually checking out his own reflection.

"Uh-uh. No way Ms. Donovan would go for a steroid case like that," said Jules.

"I beggeth to differ," said Kat, putting on her own fairly decent British accent as she nodded across the hall.

Jules looked over and saw Ms. Donovan walking slowly down the hall, pretending to thumb through some papers on her clipboard, when in reality she was secretly stealing glances at the coach. As a result, she walked right into a student in a big hurry to get somewhere. Her papers scattered everywhere.

Kat gave Jules a knowing glance. Jules shook her head in disbelief as she and Kat rushed over to help Ms. Donovan save her papers from being trampled by the horde of passing students.

"Here you go, Ms. Donovan," said Jules as she handed over a pile of crumpled documents.

"Thanks, ladies. I guess I better pay attention to where I'm going," replied Ms. Donovan.

"Tooooootally understandable," said Kat, handing over papers with a sweet smile and a knowing nod in the direction of Coach Scofield.

Embarrassed, Ms. Donovan stuffed the papers on her clipboard. "I will, uh, see you in Shakespeare Club," she said to Jules and quickly scurried away.

"Me thinketh Mistress Donovan doth crush-eth on the coach big-time," said Kat.

Despite herself, Jules joined Kat in her giggling fit.

● ● ●

The display on Kat's cell phone said 1:37 p.m. as she pushed open the front door and scanned the school parking lot for her ride. It was an early dismissal day, and she was eager to get home, but it had taken her a few minutes to pry herself away from Mr. Deevers's lecture on the importance of the isosceles triangle in everyday life.

Tonight, her dad was finally returning from his business trip. For weeks he had been in Tokyo, where his software company was setting up a system for some really big worldwide corporation. It was particularly special to have him back because it was her parents' fifteenth anniversary as well. She thought about the family dinner, their first together in a long time. She couldn't wait to see him and witness his reaction to Kat's special anniversary gift that she'd been working on all summer.

As she bounded down the steps to the curb, she hopped into the backseat of a waiting Prius. Jules was already inside.

"There you are. I was beginning to wonder if I should send out a search party," said Jules.

"Sorry I'm late, Mr. Finch," said Kat to Jules's dad in the front seat.

"Not a problem, Kat. We're in no rush. Right, Jule Box?" said Jules's father, Dale, putting the car into drive and pulling away from the curb. He was wearing his usual plaid cotton shirt, jeans, and work boots, the "official uniform" of the president of a construction company. He was so unlike Kat's dad in every way. In fact, Kat couldn't remember the last time she saw her dad in anything other than a business suit and tie. When she saw him at all, that is.

Kat liked Jules's dad, who always smelled of freshly sawed wood and called his daughter little pet names like

Jule Box and Jule O'Mine. Somehow, he always, always found time to get away from work to pick her up from school. That's another thing Kat couldn't remember about her dad—the last time he'd driven her home from school. Or *to* school, for that matter.

Kat suddenly caught herself feeling jealous, so she quickly stared out the window to avoid making eye contact with Jules, who always managed to read her mind—a downside to someone knowing you almost as long as you've known yourself.

Just then a ticket appeared in front of Kat's face. She had to cross her eyes to read it. It said:

ADMIT ONE—RENAISSANCE PLEASURE FAIRE
OCTOBER 15

She took the ticket from Jules. "What's this?" she asked.

"This is what we're doing for my fourteenth birthday!" squealed Jules. "Dad got them for us. Isn't it the best idea ever? We can all dress up like medieval characters! The Froggy Boggards will be performing, and Pilch the Storyteller is going to be there too! Oh, and Ms. Donovan says the Shakespeare Club will get to perform their sonnets on the small stage and maybe even sing a song to warm up the crowd before one of the jousts! Isn't that great? You'll be there, right?"

Kat didn't have to answer. They had been at each other's birthday parties since the Finches had invited the newly moved-in Connors family to attend Jules's Sleeping Beauty–themed second birthday party. Although that party was now a sworn secret between Kat and Jules because Jules didn't want anyone to know she had ever bought into that whole princess thing, even if she was only two at the time. Because in addition to being totally green and a vegan, Jules considered herself a feminist, and feminists didn't need guys to save them.

"Duh. Of course I'll be there. But I'm not eating any rats on a spit," joked Kat.

"You're so elitist," joked Jules back at her.

"And I'm not turning off my cell phone," said Kat.

"Will you at least put it on vibrate?"

"Okay. But that's your birthday present from me."

They both laughed as the car pulled up in front of Jules's house. The girls got out and Jules's dad said something about having to get back to the job site and seeing Jules later that evening. But Kat wasn't really listening. Instead, as the Prius pulled away, she stared open-mouthed toward Jules's large Craftsman-style home. But it wasn't the house that drew her attention. It was the totally hot-looking guy who was shooting hoops at the end of the driveway. He was tall and lanky, but very toned and tanned. His flop of brown hair swayed down over one eye but didn't seem to prevent him from hitting basket after basket. Nothing but net!

"Who is *that*?" whispered Kat to Jules.

Jules looked at Kat with disbelief. "Uh, that's Kyle. My brother. You've known him since before you could tie your shoes."

"Wow. Really? I haven't seen him all summer and he looks so, so different," marveled Kat.

"He still looks like the same annoying jock boy to me, except tanner," shrugged Jules.

"And buffer. And he's grown like three inches. Your parents weren't kidding around when they sent him to Atlanta to build those Houses for Humans that they're so into."

"Habitat for Humanity. Yeah, Kyle was pretty annoyed since all he wanted to do all summer was practice so he could try out for the freshman basketball team. But Mom and Dad are real believers in giving back to the community. I've got plenty of causes, but they thought Kyle needed some focus. So when Dad volunteered labor from his company, he volunteered Kyle too. I guess the plus side of manual labor is the manual part. He did get in pretty good shape over the summer."

"You're telling me!" said Kat.

"Uh. Yeah. Anyway, he's back now and I have to start sharing the remote again, which is a total drag," groaned Jules. "I have to get to work on my sonnet. Call me if you can't figure out that geometry stuff."

Kat watched as Jules walked up the driveway. She could hear Jules acknowledge her brother with a "Hey, loser" and him respond to her with a "How's it going, dweeb?" When Jules turned to wave good-bye to Kat just before disappearing into the house, Kyle turned too. And their eyes locked for an instant. Kyle smiled and gave Kat a nod.

Kat felt her face flush hot and red. She waved back and then turned quickly and hightailed it across the street to her own house.

She almost tripped as she tried to negotiate the stairs up to the entryway of her huge Tudor-style home in her strappy sandals with heels. But she caught herself and hoped against all hope that Kyle wasn't still watching. When she turned to look over her shoulder, she saw that he was. Embarrassed but also a little pleased, she managed to make it the rest of the way to the door without taking a header into the begonias.

As she did, her thoughts turned from Kyle and his floppy brown hair.

"Dad! Daddy! I'm home!" she yelled, the screen door slamming behind her.

Chapter 4

What Light from Yonder Laptop Breaks?

Kat entered the house, depositing her backpack in the middle of the entryway. She heard her father's voice coming from the kitchen. She dashed past the new 4K TV in the living room and arrived out of breath in the kitchen to find her mom having a heart-to-heart discussion with…a computer?

Oh joy. Another Internet video date for her parents. On their anniversary, no less. Her heart sunk for her mom.

"…and make sure you call Angela Wilson to cancel my golf date with Gene on Saturday," her father's digitized voice called out over the speakers of the computer. His image appeared in full-screen mode on her mom's laptop that she kept near the phone. Her dad continued, "That should give him plenty of time to find another partner. You know how Gene Wilson gets if he doesn't have anyone around to pretend he isn't cheating on his golf score."

Kat's mom, Trudy, nodded, dutifully taking notes on a pad set out by the computer for just this purpose.

"Shall I reschedule with the Wilsons?" Trudy said in a voice that tried to hide the fact that she was terribly disappointed. Kat watched her mom with compassion. Her mom had gotten really good at acting like all these disappointments and postponements were no biggie, but for Kat, it was harder. And it hurt. She could barely even look at her dad's image on the screen.

"Hey!" Paul's voice brightened up, catching a glimpse of Kat as she came into view of the webcam. "Is that Kat? How you doing, kiddo? Is it that late already?"

"No, Daddy," Kat said, summoning up a forced smile. "Remember today is the last Friday of the month, early dismissal day."

"Since when?" Paul Connors stepped out of camera range for a moment, coming back with a necktie draped around his neck.

"Since forever," Kat said. "Daddy, I thought you were coming home today."

"I did too, honey, but circumstances didn't allow it."

"What does that mean?" Kat said, doing a significantly worse job than her mom at hiding her disappointment.

"It means that Mr. Fujimora wants to go over the figures again with his team before he signs the contract," said Paul, executing a perfect Windsor knot on his silk necktie. Kat recognized that tie; she had helped her mom pick it out for her dad's birthday. Well, for her dad's birthday *celebration* anyway. Her dad had been in Paris or Beijing or Timbuktu or some other foreign place on the actual birthday. But like many celebrations at the Connors house, that had to be "adjusted" to fit her dad's work schedule.

Kat tried not to mind. She knew that a big part of being an international businessman like her dad was the "international" part, but it seemed like the higher he moved up in the industry, the more he was needed in Lisbon or Rome or Tegucigalpa (wherever *that* was). For a while, Kat kept a map of all the different places her dad went on business, but she had run out of thumbtacks somewhere between Paris and Abu Dhabi, and she hadn't gotten around to getting any more at the drugstore. That map was in the attic now, gathering dust alongside her American Girl tea set.

Suddenly, Kat snapped out of her funk. "Holy cow!" she said, remembering the gift. "I almost forgot! I'll be right back!"

Kat bounded up the stairs toward her room to retrieve the one thing that might salvage the day a little. "Just a minute, just a minute, just a minute!" she yelled behind her. She ran past the master bedroom, the guest room, her mom's sewing room (although she never sewed anything, as far as Kat could tell), the second guest room, and finally arrived at her own bedroom at the end of the hallway.

Jules always said that there should be a snack shop or a vending machine on the way to Kat's bedroom so that weary travelers could rest up before they finished the final leg of their journey. But that was just Jules being Jules. Their house wasn't *that* much bigger than the other houses on the cul-de-sac. True, it *was* a bit on the roomy side for just three people, but her mom did like to have her friends over for cocktail parties and stuff, and there were lots of good nooks and crannies for hide-and-seeking during sleepovers, and it was the only home Kat had ever known, and besides, Jules's house wasn't much smaller.

Jules liked to play the part of nature girl, but when it came right down to it, she had as much stuff as everybody else in this part of town. Or so Kat told herself anyway, especially after one of Jules's many sermonettes on the dangers of not recycling or the carbon footprint being left by all the barbecue parties Kat's mom threw during the summer.

Kat zipped past the seldom-used desk, just now covered with the discards from this morning's fashion decisions, and dropped to her knees and began searching under the bed. She pushed past a couple of old teddy bears (Captain

Cuddles wasn't lookin' so hot these days, she noted briefly), and…Eureka! There it was. She pulled the book out and looked at its handmade cover and note: "Kat's Annual Super-Duper Scrapbook of Memories."

Every year for the last ten years, Kat had presented a scrapbook to her parents on their anniversary, filled with what had happened in the family the previous year. True, for the first few years, it had been pretty much her mom's deal, but little by little Kat had taken over the day-to-day operations of the family scrapbooking enterprise. Even though Trudy would never admit it, Kat thought that she'd improved on some of her mom's original ideas.

She ran back into the kitchen, book in hand, smiling broadly. "Happy anniversary, Mom and Dad!" she said.

"Is that what I think it is?" said her father, peering into the webcam.

"It sure is!" said Kat cheerily.

"Well, hold it up to the screen so I can see it."

As best they could, the family paged through the scrapbook, recalling all the events of the previous twelve months. There was the picture of Kat on one of her first days of school last year, when she was just getting to know the other kids at Willkie. (Paul had been in Kuala Lumpur then.) And there was Kat and her cousin Sophie standing outside the Mall of America in Bloomington, Minnesota, on a shopping junket last fall. (Paul was in Dallas for that one.)

And another picture of Kat around Christmastime, when Paul was flying back from Shanghai. She was building a snowman outside the house with Jules. ("Snow citizen" is what Jules preferred to call it.) And was that Kyle all bundled up in the background with the snowblower? Even in that down jacket, he did look kind of hot back then too, come to think of it.

"Wow, Kat, this has got to be your best one yet!" Paul said.

"Well, remember it *was* Mom's idea. She started this whole tradition," Kat said, giving her mom a peck on the cheek. Kat had noticed her mom had turned quiet as she and her dad were looking through the scrapbook.

"Awww heck," said her dad, "what am I doing here? Kat's not the only one with a present. I've got something very special for my lovely wife." Kat watched as her dad disappeared for a moment, and then he returned with…a pad and pen? Kat looked at her mother and noticed the fleeting look of disappointment in her eyes. He hadn't actually shopped for a present at all.

Here we go again, thought Kat.

"I'm writing down a number," Paul said smiling. "And Trudy, I'm going to be very disappointed if I get home and you and your girlfriends haven't gone out to the spa and completely pampered yourselves and spent every last cent of it." He held up the piece of paper to the webcam. Kat had to look at the number twice. Then she turned and looked at her mom, whose eyes went from disappointed to lighting up like two searchlights cutting through a foggy morning.

And there it is, the buy-off. Gross.

"You're kidding, right?" said Trudy. "It's so, so extravagant!"

"Nothing less than you deserve," said Paul, smiling. "You just call Wendy and the other girls and have some fun. Happy anniversary, honey."

Kat's mom let loose such a high-pitched squeal of delight that Kat was sure owls from miles around would be swooping at their home any second now, looking for the wounded pack of field mice that had emitted such a sound.

There was a little more chitchat (very little, he had to get to an important meeting) where Kat dutifully said, "Yes, Daddy," a few times when he pestered her about her grades. Then they said their good-byes.

• • •

She turned to her mom, who was already on her cell phone checking her calendar for an available date for her spa day. It irritated Kat. She contemplated telling her mom she shouldn't let her dad back out on her like that. It was their anniversary, for Pete's sake! But she knew her mom would give her "the speech"—the one about how hard her dad worked to give them this nice life and how there were kids who would be twice as happy with half as much. Besides, if her husband wanted to do something nice for her, who was a fourteen-year-old girl to tell her mother anything different anyway? Or words to that effect.

Instead Kat simply said, "Happy anniversary, Mom. I love you." Her mom gave her a quick smile but didn't respond. She couldn't. She was on the phone with the spa, booking her anniversary gift.

• • •

Later, back in her room, Kat pushed the incident out of her mind, the same way she pushed the discarded clothes off her desk, and grabbed her own laptop. She had homework to do. Something about those triangles, she supposed. But she figured that could wait. Instead, she logged on to the Internet to check her IMs and email. A girl needs to have her priorities straight.

Let's see. A link to some online petition from Jules.

Whatever. An embedded video of the *cutest* little puppies chasing a balloon around somebody's backyard. *Watch that later.* A couple of comments at her blog site thanking her for her article picking the cutest tops for fall. *My pleasure.* An email from something called Glitter Girl declaring, "You're a winner!" *Probably spam.* Finally, there was a pile of various other emails from friends who hadn't convinced their parents to give them unlimited texting yet. *Ho-hum.*

As Kat logged on to her own blog site, girlstylepatrol.com, and thought about what to write for today's entry, she peered out the window across the cul-de-sac to Jules's house. Jules was sitting on the front steps reading a book (sonnets for Ms. Donovan, Kat assumed) while her mom sat one step above her and braided Jules's hair. Her mom was a busy lawyer for a nonprofit law firm downtown that helped low-income people with legal problems, but somehow she always managed to be home in time for dinner.

In the driveway, Kyle and his dad were engaged in a game of "Horse" or "Pig" or whatever you call that game when you have to make the shot that the guy before you just made. Jules's dad wasn't a great player, but Jules and her mom would clap loudly when he managed to get it in the basket. Mr. Finch played along by bowing extravagantly every time he made a shot and passing out high fives all around to his adoring fans on the stoop.

Kat smiled wistfully. It looked nice. It looked like a family.

Kat sighed for a moment, then turned away and started to type. And with every keystroke, her blues began slowly fading and turning into the loveliest shade of pink!

Tonight's topic: Let us all now praise fabulous accessories!

Chapter 5

Some are Born Great
(Others Watch Greatness Drive Up in a Really Cool Pink Convertible)

Bounce. Dip. Bounce. Steal a glance. Swish. Bounce. Paint.
Bounce. Dip. Bounce. Steal a glance. Swish. Bounce. Paint.

Kat was really enjoying this. So much, in fact, that it made her wonder if she hadn't gone a little loopy. Sitting there on her front porch on this Saturday afternoon, secretly stealing glances at Kyle across the street shooting hoops while painting her toenails a fabulous shade of pink—"Aphrodite's Pink Nightie" it was called.

The bounce of the basketball. The dip of the nail polish. A second bounce. A stolen glance as *Swish!* the ball made it through the hoop, followed by another bounce as Kyle retrieved it and she ran the polish over a toenail. It was Zen almost, the rhythm of it all, and she was enjoying every second of it. Until—

"We've been sitting on your porch for an hour. Can we please go *do* something?" moaned Jules dramatically as she bent backward as far as she could over the banister of Kat's front porch to the point where she was looking upside down at Kat. Clearly, Jules wasn't finding this experience nearly as Zen as Kat.

"I *am* doing something. I'm doing my nails," Kat replied as she ran the tiny brush over her big toe.

"Please. Since when do you *do* your nails? You've always had them *done*. You're just using this as an excuse to watch Kyle."

Even as Kat started to deny it, she accidentally painted the knuckle of her big toe because her eyes had been on Kyle's shirtless torso instead of on her feet.

She looked up at Jules, who was giving her a smug smile—although upside down it looked like a freaky sort of frown. Kat continued doing exactly what she was doing.

"Fine. Then I'll take matters into my own hands. Kyle!" yelled Jules as she righted herself. "Will you pleeeease put on a shirt so Kat will stop—"

Mortified, Kat jumped up, completely forgetting her wet toes, and clamped her hand over Jules's mouth.

"Don't you dare!" she hissed and begged at the same time. Jules, whose voice was muffled, laughed as she wriggled to get out from Kat's stronghold. But there are few things stronger than a fourteen-year-old girl who absolutely does not want her crush revealed.

Just then the Connors's black Range Rover pulled into

the driveway. Out of the car bounced Trudy, looking positively pink and glowing from a day at the most elegant spa in town—the kind of place where they have sliced cucumbers on ice for your eyes! And all the free bananas you can eat.

"That was absolutely sublime!" she exclaimed to what seemed to be the whole neighborhood.

I guess she liked her anniversary present, thought Kat.

Kat let go of Jules and they watched as Trudy's group of "ladies who lunch" also stepped out of the car. There were two of them and, in addition to looking like clones of Trudy, they also sported the same pampered, refreshed, and glowing look. It struck Kat by the way they followed her mother and hung on her every word that they were a lot like Zoe and Darcy. In fact, Kat got the weird sense of seeing her future in this trio, and frankly, it creeped her out.

"Trudy. You must thank Paul from me. I have been so exfoliated I'm convinced they've unearthed the original skin I was born with...twenty-nine years ago!" joked Wendy, Trudy's best friend since college who was at least forty years old.

The trio laughed hard at Wendy's little "age" joke. Too hard, judging by the looks on Kat's and Jules's faces. The girls clearly didn't think it was all that funny. Not only because they'd heard that joke so many times before, but because twenty-nine still seemed old to them. Kind of ancient, in fact.

Wendy and Johanna, Trudy's other friend, waved their good-byes and went to their cars parked at the curb. Trudy waved back and then turned to the girls.

"Hello, ladies. And how was your day?" Trudy asked merrily, casually tossing her keys into her purse. But before they could answer, Trudy went on.

"We had the absolute best time at the Green Ivy Spa. We indulged in every treatment under the sun. Spared no expense. Or should I say, your father spared no expense. But now I'm exhausted. That deep-tissue massage—I feel positively like a wet noodle. I think I'm going to take a quick catnap before dinner. How does takeout from Kabuki sound? Order in thirty minutes. Wake me when the food gets here."

Trudy kissed Kat on the forehead and went inside, her Jimmy Choo sandals clacking across the porch and fading into the house.

With Trudy and her friends gone, Kat suddenly realized how very quiet it was. Too quiet. She looked over at Jules's driveway. There was no sign of Kyle anywhere. Sometime during the arrival of the whirling dervish that was her mother, he had given up his practice and gone inside. Bummer.

Kat turned to Jules. "Want to stay for dinner?"

"Sure. As long as there's at least one dish that doesn't include an animal sacrifice."

"I'll get the menu."

• • •

While Jules waited for Kat to return with her food options, she picked up the bottle of polish. She looked around to make sure no one was looking, slipped her left foot out of her Converse Hi-Top, and painted one toe. She wasn't one to do her toenails. She thought it was frivolous and a lame attempt to get boys' attention. In fact, she'd given Kat a whole big speech about how, if a boy liked her, he'd have to like her for who she was on the inside and not the color that was painted on her feet. But she had to admit, even if it was only to herself, it looked kind of cute. She quickly did the rest of the toes on her foot and stretched it out in front of her to better admire her handiwork.

Just then, a pink Mercedes convertible pulled into her field of vision, right where she had been staring at her toot-sies. *Aphrodite Pink Nightie, in fact*, thought Jules, noting the car was almost exactly the same shade of pink as what she had just painted on her toenails. Jules quickly stuck her foot back in her sneaker as the car door opened and she watched a super long, trim-calved leg in spiked heels make its appearance. Attached to this leg, which looked like it could have been featured in a fashion magazine, was a woman who looked like she had just stepped out of one.

Wearing a black pencil skirt, a tight white sweater with pink marabou at the collar, and black sunglasses studded with rhinestones that matched her handbag was a tall woman in her twenties. She had sleek blond hair that seemed to move in one piece—like you see in those shampoo commercials—and perfect skin. In fact, everything about her looked perfect. She walked directly up to Jules, who was sitting on the step, and stood over her.

"I'm looking for Katherine Connors," said the woman. She slid her sunglasses down her nose to get a better look at Jules, revealing her piercing blue eyes.

"You can't be her."

Jules didn't know what she meant by that comment or how she could possibly know she wasn't Kat, but she immediately didn't care for this woman.

"I'm Kat Connors," said Kat from behind the screen door. She stepped onto the porch with the Kabuki menu in her hand. The woman gave Kat a quick once-over. She apparently liked what she saw because she broke into a gleaming smile so white that there was something distinctly fake about it.

"Ah, yes. Kat! I'm Chelsea Ambrose. So nice to finally meet you," she said as she extended her hand.

Kat looked confused. Was she supposed to know this woman?

"I sent you an email a few days ago. I represent Glitter Girl products?"

Kat vaguely remembered the email she had clicked past, thinking it was some kind of spam.

"Oh yeah. I saw that. But I didn't think it was anything important."

"Not important? Oh no, honey. On the contrary. It may be *the* most important thing ever to happen in your life. You see, you've been chosen!"

• • •

Trudy had not been happy to be awakened early from her catnap. But her mood quickly changed when she learned why Kat had prematurely lifted the blackout mask from her eyes. She'd gone from cranky to giddy in about thirty seconds flat. And now, at this very moment, she was flitting around the center island in their kitchen arranging cut crystal glasses and a matching pitcher filled with iced tea on a silver tray for their guest.

Chelsea was perched on the edge of the huge overstuffed sofa in the family room, maintaining her picture-perfect posture. Kat sat directly across from her. Jules sat in the corner, cross-legged on a raised hearth by the fireplace, an observer to the scene that was unfolding.

"My Kat? Chosen out of how many girls?" asked Trudy as she set down the tray and began pouring a glass for Chelsea.

"Thousands. Tens of thousands, actually," said Chelsea, taking the tiniest sip before putting the glass down on the table. She didn't touch the petite scone that Trudy had put on a plate next to her glass.

"You see, as part of the marketing of our new Glitter Girl line of products, we've picked fifty Alpha Girls, one from each state…"

"Alpha Girl? What's an Alpha Girl?" asked Kat.

"Well," began Chelsea, "they—*you*—are the trendsetters. Alpha Girls are girls who are ahead of the curve when it comes to what's hot. Girls who the other girls look to for guidance on fashion, music…well, almost anything that matters to girls at this age."

"Global warming?" asked Jules in her most innocent-sounding voice.

Chelsea turned, looking surprised that Jules had spoken. Surprised that she was even there, in fact.

"Things that matter to *normal* girls," amended Chelsea, giving Jules a look that would have melted the polar ice caps.

Kat shot Jules a look of her own that told her to cool it.

"Well, that is definitely my Kat. She has always had a flair for fashion. She gets that from me, you know," said Trudy.

"Well, that's certainly obvious," said Chelsea in her most flattering tone. Trudy ate it up.

"What do I have to do, you know, to be an Alpha Girl?" asked Kat.

"You don't have to do anything. Just be yourself. Of course as part of being chosen, you get to throw a fabulous slumber party for a handful of girls of your choosing—with a little input from me, naturally. And you and the girls you select will get the first chance at a whole new line of Glitter Girl products that feature all the latest trends in fashion, electronics, and makeup. And all of it is yours to keep!"

"To keep?" squealed Kat. "And all I have to do is have the slumber party?"

"Certainly we would hope you take the items to school. Show them to the other kids. It's a form of advertising. Also, you would write about the items on your blog."

"*If* she wanted to," clarified Jules.

"Of course. That's goes without saying," said Chelsea. This girl was getting on her nerves.

"Well, if I really liked something, I suppose I could," said Kat. Her blog was like her diary. And she never, ever expressed anything but her true feelings in it.

"I've no doubt you'll adore our line. Oh, and did I mention that one of the fifty girls, the one girl we decide best embodies the spirit of Glitter Girl, will be chosen to be the Face of Glitter Girl for the kickoff ad campaign? We're talking print ads. TV commercials. Even having your face on some of the packaging. "

Now it was Trudy who squealed. So loudly, in fact, that it made everyone wince. Trudy grabbed Kat and began bouncing up and down in excitement.

"Oh Kat! Imagine that. Your face on the packaging. Like those movie stars all over the cosmetic section of the drugstore! I'm so proud of you. I knew you were always a leader like me! I knew you had it in you to be an Alpha Girl!"

Kat couldn't deny it. She was pretty darned excited too. Getting chosen out of thousands of girls. That a big company in Los Angeles cared enough about her opinions to come all the way to Carmel to talk to her. That had to be an honor, right? And all that free, cool stuff. She could help decide what would become popular or not. She started jumping up and down with her mom.

"So, how exactly did Glitter Girl access all this information about Kat, you know, to determine if she was an Alpha Girl?" Jules spoke up.

Kat and Trudy stopped their bouncing. All eyes turned to Jules. Chelsea looked at Jules with that ice-cap-melting stare again. Who was this frumpy little girl wearing the Converse Hi-Tops? And why was she sitting in this room questioning her, Chelsea Ambrose?

"I'm sorry. Who are you, sweetie?" asked Chelsea in a sweet drawl that masked her dislike.

"That's Jules," answered Kat. "She's my best friend."

"Yeah, I'm her best friend. And my mom's a lawyer and all this accessing of personal information, it just doesn't sound too legal if you ask me."

"I can assure you it is totally legal or we wouldn't have been able to do it," Chelsea said, looking at Trudy, irritated that this little troublemaker with an unflattering haircut might have raised some red flags with one of her Alpha Girls' mothers. This was something Chelsea had not considered and something that could really cause problems for her grand scheme.

But when Trudy raised no objection and instead started

shooting out a string of her own apologies because she'd forgotten to put the Splenda on the tray, Chelsea knew she was in the clear. They drank an iced-tea toast to their new Alpha Girl, Kat, and all seemed well.

Still, Chelsea felt a niggling of concern as she glanced over at the shaggy-haired Jules in the corner, refusing to raise a toast. Best friend, huh? If there's one thing Chelsea knew about best friends, they could have influence. And judging from the looks of this girl, that could spell trouble.

. . .

Kat fell back on the king-sized, pillow-top mattress in her bedroom and stared at the ceiling in shock.

"Can you believe it? Me? Chosen by Glitter Girl?" asked Kat.

"What's not to believe?" said Jules who was sprawled over a zebra-striped beanbag chair. "I mean, you have a real sense of style."

Kat shot up and looked at Jules. "Really, you think so?"

"Sure. It's not my taste, but yeah, you've always dressed really cool, and you've always seemed to know what to wear and how to wear it. I mean, since forever. And tons of girls read your blog. A lot of girls really envy you."

"What girls envy me?" asked Kat.

Jules shifted uncomfortably, knowing she had felt that

way a time or two. Not about Kat's fashion sense. She couldn't care less about that stuff. But about how easily Kat could talk to people and make friends. Jules always had to try so hard. *Too hard sometimes*, she thought.

"I don't know. But trust me, they do," said Jules, who quickly changed the subject. "Hey. I have a question for you. What are you going to do if they give you stuff and you don't like it?"

"What do you mean?" asked Kat.

"I mean, you've always been your own girl with your own tastes. You've never copied other girls. That's what's so cool about you. But now, what if Glitter Girl gives you stuff you don't like?"

Kat hadn't considered this. After all, how could something so absolutely therocious-sounding as Glitter Girl be...lame? Nah. No way. They *had* looked into her tastes and picked her, so they had to know she would like the stuff they gave her.

"I'll like it."

"But what if you don't?"

"Then I'll say I don't. They want my opinion, right?" said Kat, irritated.

Jules shrugged, put in her earbuds, and closed her eyes, nodding her head to unheard music.

Ugh! Upset by the fact that Jules had managed to make her worry on what should be one of the happiest days of her life, Kat stomped over to the computer and clicked on her blog. She began typing.

Guess what? Apparently I'm an Alpha Girl...

As usual, with each stroke of the keyboard, her worries began to melt away.

Chapter 6

The Stuff That Glitter Girls Are Made Of

"Have you heard about Kat Connors?"

"Yeah! She got picked by this big fashion company to try out a bunch of their new stuff…for free!"

"OMG! She is *so* lucky!"

"I heard she gets to invite twenty girls to a slumber party, and they get free cool stuff too!"

"That would be soooo awesome."

"Totally!"

"I hope she chooses me."

"I hope she chooses me!"

"I hope she chooses me!!!"

By Monday morning, the halls of Willkie Junior High School were abuzz with the news of Kat's good fortune. When Jules's dad dropped Kat and Jules off in front of the school, you could feel it. All eyes were on Kat. If before she had been a popular girl at school, this cemented her position as simply *legendary*. She was now on the Mount Rushmore of Popular, and she could sense it better than anyone.

"I haven't seen this much excitement at school since the day those drug-sniffing dogs came last year for that assembly during Red Ribbon Week," Jules said as they walked up the sidewalk to the school entrance.

"Those dogs were adorable," Kat said. "And so well-trained!"

"Just like Zoe and Darcy, only without the fleas," said Jules.

"Ha, ha," said Kat sarcastically as the girls turned the corner in the hallway toward homeroom. Speak of the devil, as the girls approached their lockers outside the classroom, Zoe and Darcy were already there.

"Like…OMG! OMG! OMG!" bubbled Zoe, unable to contain her excitement, "This is like totally, like *awesome*!"

"It's absolutely prepositional!" Darcy said, misusing yet another word and giving Kat a big hug as soon as she came within arm's reach. "I can't wait for the slumber party! And all that free stuff!"

"Yeah," Kat said, wriggling out of the grasp of the slightly overenthusiastic Darcy. "It will be great. But I've got to figure out *who* to invite."

"Like, no duh," said Zoe, taking Kat's arm and walking with her into first period. "You don't want to waste any of the invitations on people who aren't, shall we say, 'Glitter

Girl material.'" Zoe shot Jules a look over her shoulder that left no doubt who that comment was intended for. Jules responded in the mature manner that only comes from being raised by a lawyer, schooled in the fine points of debate. She stuck out her tongue at Zoe.

Jules usually took the things that Darcy and Zoe said about as seriously as she followed the NBA (in other words, not at all), but Zoe's snide "Glitter Girl material" remark put Jules in a seriously bad mood all morning. She found her mind drifting all the way through Mr. Adams's first period lecture on photosynthesis.

Adams was as boring as dirt, but usually Jules was able to muster the self-control to actually pay attention to his lectures. Today, however, she found herself looking across the classroom to where Kat and Darcy were sitting under a scale model of the solar system. (Darn Mr. Adams and his stupid seating chart!) Kat wouldn't actually *not* invite her, would she? The whole Glitter Girl thing was stupid and superficial and all, but still...*Focus, Jules, focus!*

"Plants absorb light primarily using the pigment chlorophyll, which is the reason most plants have a green color," Adams droned on, pointing to some sort of graph on the SMART Board in the front of the room. "Besides chlorophyll, plants also use pigments such as carotenes and xanthophylls."

Kat, on the other hand, wasn't even *trying* to think about photosynthesis. While there was nothing particularly unique about that, this time Kat's daydreams had purpose. She kept thinking about the last forty-eight hours and the sound of the basketball going through the net when Kyle shot it, and how cool Chelsea's car was, and how *different* everyone at school had seemed that morning.

Choosing just twenty girls to go to this party was going to be so hard. It would almost be better if she only had to choose three. BFFs only. Fine. But twenty! That meant she'd have to go outside her little circle of close friends and choose some girls that maybe she didn't even know that well or (gasp!) didn't even like that much.

Well, so be it, she thought. "To whom much is given, much is expected," she said to herself, which was either a quote from the Bible or from Frodo Baggins in *The Lord of the Rings*; she could never keep it straight in her head. All she knew was she had to come up with a list for Chelsea by the end of the day and it wasn't going to be easy.

"Miss Connors!" Mr. Adams's gravelly voice broke up her daydreaming.

"What page are we on?" said Kat reflexively.

"No, Miss Connors, much as we'd love to hear you opine on the life of chloroplasts, that won't be necessary at this time," said Mr. Adams peering over his glasses at a recently delivered note from the principal's office. "Your presence is requested at Principal Neimeyer's office."

Kat looked at him as if he had suddenly started speaking Cherokee. The office? Principal Neimeyer? What in the *world* could this be about?

"I didn't do anything!" Kat protested.

"I don't recall saying that you did," said Adams in his typical way of saying a lot while at the same time saying nothing at all.

"But..."

"I'm sorry, Ms. Connors. Your 'but' will have to wait," said Mr. Adams, not realizing how his comment sounded to the ears of adolescents, who all started snickering behind their textbooks. "Get to the office. Now."

Kat got up and slinked toward the door. Well, as much as one could slink when the eyes of thirty-one eighth graders were fastened on her.

"Mr. Adams, can she bring her 'but' back to class later?" asked Gustavo Reyes, who could always be counted on for a dumb joke.

The class erupted into laughter, and Kat turned a shade of red that hadn't been invented yet.

"That's enough, Mr. Reyes," said Mr. Adams, turning

back to the SMART Board. "Now, let's move on to the next slide."

As she reached the door, Kat shot Jules a look. Jules, who was as in the dark about this as Kat was, could only shrug her shoulders, as if to say, "Beats me."

As Kat walked through the empty halls toward the principal's office on the first floor, she started to think about her time in junior high. She thought back to how some of those creepy ninth graders had given them such a hard time on "rookie day" last year, but then she remembered what her mom told her at the time: "The only thing worse than being picked on is being ignored."

Well, she certainly wasn't being ignored today. Why, even some of this year's ninth graders seemed to walk a couple of steps behind her. Funny how word got around so quickly, but then again, it wasn't sooo funny considering that Kat's blog was getting thousands of hits every month. Her mom told her that, in her day, a girl would simply *die* if that many people read her diary and knew her innermost thoughts, but Kat wondered what was the point of even *having* thoughts if you didn't share them online. Her mom grew up in the Stone Age, the ever-loving Stone Age.

She entered the principal's office and was waved in by Mrs. Henry, the school secretary, who was scratching her head and looking at the directions for a new copy machine that was now taking up the lion's share of the outer office.

"They're waiting for you, hon. Just go on in," Mrs. Henry said.

They? thought Kat. That didn't sound good.

The door to Principal Neimeyer's office was ajar. Kat walked in slowly.

"Close it, please," said the principal, sitting at his desk.

Kat turned to close the door and found herself face-to-face with a very stern-looking Ms. Donovan, who stood by the door with her arms folded, looking down her nose at Kat as if she had questioned the quality of *A Midsummer Night's Dream.*

"Have a seat, Katherine," said Ms. Donovan in a way that Kat knew definitely was *not* good. Nobody called her Katherine except people who didn't know her or her mom when she was *really* mad.

"Is there something you wanted to see me about?" Kat asked.

Principal Neimeyer glanced at Ms. Donovan in a way that told Kat he had probably been forced into this meeting too.

"Er, this Glitter Girl," he said. "Are you familiar with this outfit?"

"Oh," said Kat, "that."

"Yes, that," said Ms. Donovan. "There's been endless whispering and chitchatting about it in my class. I've had to fight for attention all morning."

More than usual, you mean? thought Kat, but she knew much better than to say it.

"Katherine, this is serious business!" said Ms. Donovan, who was obviously steamed about the whole thing. "Girls are not focused on anything today but some silly sleepover at your house on Saturday."

"Yeah, I kinda have to choose twenty girls to invite, and we all get makeovers and electronics and all kinds of free stuff from Glitter Girl. By the way, have you ever considered highlights? They would really bring out your eyes."

"Don't change the subject! Do you see what this is doing to the girls, Kat?" Ms. Donovan said. "Don't you see what Glitter Girl wants from you?"

"They just want us to try some of their products. You know, lip gloss and stuff."

"It starts with lip gloss, but do you know where it ends?"

"Eyeliner?" said Kat, making her best guess.

Principal Neimeyer nodded. Sounded reasonable to him.

"No, Kat, not eyeliner. It ends with jealousy and back-biting, and some girls being 'in' and some girls being excluded, and nobody even remembering why they cared so much about it in the first place."

"Please, Ms. Donovan. I'm fourteen. I think I can handle throwing a little party without causing World War III."

"That's what Lady Capulet said to Juliet!" shouted Ms. Donovan, which must have meant something. What, Kat had no idea.

"Owen, you talk to her. Obviously I'm not getting through." Ms. Donovan gave Neimeyer her most exasperated expression.

"Uh. Listen, Miss Connors," said Principal Neimeyer, playing nervously with a pencil. "It's all, uh, well and good that you're having this slumber party, but I can't have my school turned into chaos. As you know, as your principal, I'm not here to create disorder. I'm here to preserve it!"

"Uh, don't you mean you're here to preserve *order*?"

"No. I mean yes!" He turned to Ms. Donovan. "Are we done here, Ms. Donovan? I need to head over to the lunchroom. Mrs. Brandeis says there's some problem with the latest delivery of Tater Tots."

"Look, Kat, all we're saying is that we have to be careful not to let this thing get out of hand," said Ms. Donovan, calmer now. "I've seen how girls can treat each other with things like these, and believe me, it's no fun to be left out."

Never having been left out of *anything*, Kat would have to take Ms. Donovan's word for it. But knowing Ms. Donovan, Kat wouldn't be surprised if she knew that topic a little *too* well.

"Don't worry, Ms. Donovan. We're not going to make a big deal about it. It'll be over before you know it, and by the time it happens, everybody else will have forgotten about it."

"Good! Make sure about it," said Mr. Neimeyer. "Now, get back to the cafeteria, er, I mean class."

Kat politely exited the office and with great effort managed NOT to roll her eyes until she got into the hallway. Geez Louise! Adults get worked up over the smallest things.

Back in the office, Mr. Neimeyer grabbed an enormous set of keys from his desk and headed to the door.

"I'll keep you posted," said Ms. Donovan. "We've got to nip this thing in the bud."

"What's that? Oh, yes. Absolutely. I agree completely. By the way," said Mr. Neimeyer as he reached for the doorknob, "she's right."

"Who is?"

"That girl who was just here. She was right about the highlights. They would look quite stunning."

Ms. Donovan sighed. "Et tu, Mr. Neimeyer?"

It must have meant something. What, he had no idea.

• • •

Kat managed to survive the next four hours without incident, although she did notice that the usual circle around
her at lunchtime was considerably larger than normal. She
burst out of class when the three o'clock bell rang and
joined Jules at their lockers.

"Come on," she said, "we're going to meet Darcy and
Zoe at Sip N' Suds and try to figure out who to invite to
this party." The Sip N' Suds was a root-beer bar near the
school that also doubled as a laundromat.

"Can't," said Jules matter-of-factly. "Today's Monday.
Shakespeare Club."

"Oh, that's right. Well, maybe you could drop by after.
I'm sure we'll be there for a while."

"Maybe. I'll text you."

"You *want* to go, though, right?"

"To Sip N' Suds? Now, why wouldn't I want to go
watch someone's underwear tumble around in a dryer
while slurping on a root-beer float? No, thanks. I'll stick
with Sonnets N' Soliloquies."

With that, Jules disappeared into a sea of teenage performers, playwrights, and poets. Shakespeare people.
Her people.

• • •

As far as Kat was concerned, the Sip N' Suds was the most therocious place ever invented. There was a bank of washers and dryers on one side of the store that would be buzzing with single people from the apartment complex next door, fluffing and folding and trying to make dates with each other. And on the other side there was a root-beer bar and a bunch of comfy sofas with board games and a big-screen TV and even an old-fashioned jukebox with real records in it.

Kat didn't know how much the owners made off their coin laundry business, but since the Sip N' Suds was just across the street, the kids at Willkie gravitated there on a daily basis. It was a lot better place than *the library* to hang out after a practice or rehearsal while you were waiting for your mom to pick you up. Plus, Anastasia, the old Russian lady who ran the place, would sometimes give Kat and her friends a free root-beer float for being good customers. It was here that Kat, Darcy, and Zoe were flopped on the couch, paging through last year's yearbook, the *Willkie Wolfpack*.

"What about Maeve Finnegan?" said Kat. "She seems kind of cool."

"OMG. Her hair is soooo red," said Zoe, grabbing the book from Darcy. "It's like Elmo red."

"Elmo has a goldfish named Dorothy," said Darcy randomly. Kat and Zoe just ignored her.

"So Maeve has red hair," said Kat. "Is she in or out?"

"Well, personally I think red hair is out," said Zoe, which came as a bit of a surprise to the redheaded Darcy sitting next to her.

Kat shrugged her shoulders, "You decide about Maeve. I don't know her that well."

"Out!" said Zoe without the least bit of hesitation.

"How many girls do we have so far?" asked Kat.

Zoe counted up the names she had written on her napkin. "Nine for-sures and three maybes, not counting us."

"This is soooo hard!" moaned Kat, now upside down on the sofa and playing with her hair. "I wish we could just invite everyone! Who's next?"

Darcy looked at the next picture in the yearbook. "Penny Fong."

"Ha. Don't think so," said Zoe. "Math Club girl. Fat chance."

"What?" said Kat. "Jules is in the Math Club."

"Exactly!" said Zoe.

"Yeah, she might know what a Gaussian integer is, but I ask you, can she tell a pair of gauchos from capris?" said Darcy.

"Okay, Darce, you're scaring me," said Kat, all the while secretly wondering *what* a Gaussian integer was, and how the usually airheaded Darcy knew about them in the first place.

On it went for well over an hour. Zoe and Darcy seemed to have something to say about every one of the girls in the *Wolfpack*, and not a lot of it was good. This one had crooked teeth, and that one had parents that never let her spend money, and this other one was definitely *not* Glitter Girl material (a phrase that came up more than once). Kat wasn't a fan of the snarkiness, and she had to put her foot down more than a few times—it was her party, after all. Finally they had a list of names that everyone could agree on.

"Okay," said Kat. "That makes sixteen. With the three of us and Jules, of course, we've got our twenty."

"Wait a minute!" said Zoe. "You're not *actually* thinking of inviting Jules to this party, are you?"

Kat had never actually considered *not* inviting her. "Why not?" Kat said. "We've been besties since like forever. She's come to every slumber party I've ever had."

"Kat," said Zoe seriously, "We're not saying you can't still be her friend or anything. But just think about it. This party is different. Have you seen her wardrobe? And those shoes?"

"Yeah. It's like she's socially *detonated,*" Darcy agreed about something. Kat and Zoe weren't sure what.

"Okay, maybe some of her wardrobe choices are a little—"

"Lame?" interrupted Zoe.

"Different," corrected Kat. "But they're kind of cool in their own way. For her."

Zoe straightened up a bit in her seat. "Kat. Look at it this way. You used to have a flip phone, right?"

"Yeah, so?"

"So you move on. You *evolve.*"

"I don't know," Kat said uncertainly. "Jules is a person, not a flip phone."

"Exactly. She's the flip phone of friends! And you, you're tomorrow's version of the iPhone. Anyway, what do you think that Chelsea person would say about you inviting Jules?"

Oh, gee. Kat had almost forgotten about Chelsea. She and Jules hadn't exactly gotten off to a great start the other day. And Jules *did* seem to think the whole thing was lame in the first place. But still…this was Jules they were talking about here.

Kat stared across the room, lost in thought. She watched as a load of whites tumbled around in one of the dryers. Tossed in among the T-shirts and, ew, underwear (Jules was right) was a single purple blouse, which must have been the only colored thing that needed washing in that load. Kat couldn't take her eyes off that purple blouse as it moved up and down in the dryer. It *did* look out of place. But still...

Chapter 7

Much Ado about Pink Tickets

Kat was up even before the alarm clock went off, which was really rare for her because sleep was one of her absolute favorite things, next to shopping the sales at Forever 21 and watching zombie movies. The way those zombies lumbered around really cracked her up.

This is the day, she thought as she checked her look in the mirror. Her bangs were giving her a little trouble this morning. That annoying cowlick she inherited from her dad just wasn't responding to anything, not even the industrial-strength gel she got at the beauty supply store after reading it was the one Angelina Jolie uses. Oh well. She wasn't going to let it get to her. Not today. No siree. Because today was Wednesday, Ticket Day, and she was sure she felt just as excited to pass them out as the girls at school must be feeling to find out *who* exactly was getting one.

Kat saw herself as a little like Willy Wonka from one of her favorite childhood books, *Charlie and the Chocolate*

Factory. And she was absolutely *convinced* that being the giver-outerer of the golden tickets—or, in this case, the shiny, hot pink, rhinestone-studded tickets that Chelsea had supplied her with—was a heckuva lot better than being the receiver.

There was a certain power to it that made her feel all, well, powerful. She sure wouldn't want to be one of the girls who got passed up. For a fleeting moment she had a sick feeling in the pit of her stomach, thinking about the girls who wouldn't be chosen, but she quickly pushed it aside. "Not everyone has what it takes," as her mother often said.

She picked up the stack of tickets and carefully placed them in her backpack, her feeling of excitement rising again. She put a quick spritz of hairspray on her bangs in a final futile attempt to tame them and bounded down the stairs.

• • •

As Kat slipped into the waiting Prius, that sick feeling returned. Jules greeted her with an anxious smile.

"Hey."

"Hey," Kat responded, fumbling with the hem of her skirt to avoid eye contact. She still hadn't talked to Jules about the fact that she wasn't getting one of the tickets. Not that she felt she needed to. After all, Jules wouldn't want to come to the slumber party. She'd made it clear she thought the whole thing was superficial and stupid and a big, fat waste of life. It definitely wasn't her scene.

So why did Kat feel so guilty about it? It's not like she and Jules did absolutely everything together. Well, not lately anyway. Especially not since they hit junior high. Didn't Jules have her Math Club and Shakespeare Club, which Kat wasn't a part of? Surely Jules wouldn't care in the least that she wasn't going to be included in a Glitter Girl party.

"So today's the big day, huh?" asked Jules, trying to sound casual but not doing a very good job of it.

"Huh?" responded Kat, shocked out of her rationalizations.

"The tickets. You're giving out the tickets today?"

"Oh, yeah. Yeah, I am," said Kat, also trying to sound casual but also not doing a very good job of it. "I'm going to have to keep it on the down low, though, and probably pass them out after school. Ms. Donovan's all worried about hurt feelings and stuff. Like people are really going to care about a silly slumber party. Right? Uh, anyway, you don't have to wait for me after school, if you don't want. I can walk."

And there it was. Kat had put it out there without actually saying it. She even let herself believe that Jules's silence for the rest of the ride to school meant she was okay with it.

• • •

If the hallways were abuzz the day Kat walked into school after being chosen by Glitter Girl, today they were positively chaotic. Girls everywhere were bouncing around with a sense of anticipation she hadn't seen since the time everybody's favorite singer, Troy Cousins, did a concert at the White Oak Mall. Except when Troy made his appearance, there were shrieks and screaming and crying. Kat's classmate Savannah Lee had her usual fainting spell, which she had been doing since moving from Atlanta in the middle of second grade. She said it was a "Southern" thing. Secretly, Kat thought it was more of a "get attention" thing.

The moment Kat walked in, instead of shrieks, there was utter silence. All eyes fell on her, and for the first time in her life, the attention made her a little uncomfortable. She wasn't sure why. Maybe because she let herself think for just a second that Ms. Donovan might be right. Someone might get their feelings hurt.

But then suddenly the talking started up again. Girls, lots she didn't even know, were saying good morning to her and saying how cool she looked and how pretty her hair was, even though her bangs were clearly not cooperating!

Even the boys, who weren't looking to get a ticket, were giving her special attention. The seventh-grade boys who were usually too shy to talk to her and instead watched her through dreamy eyes as she walked through the halls. The eighth-grade boys, boys her own age, who sometimes mustered the guts to toss her a hello or buy her milk at lunch. But best of all, the ninth-grade boys—those boys on the verge of high school and shaving and driving cars—those boys who normally reserved all their attention for girls their own age, for girls who were out of training bras and already shaving their legs, were definitely sending the vibes her way. Some were nodding; some said hello.

Kat floated to her locker, because that's exactly what this moment felt like—floating on a cloud.

"OMG!" exclaimed Zoe, coming right up to Kat's locker. "Do you believe this? Positively everyone is talking about the invitations. I mean, I must have gotten a hundred texts last night asking if I knew who you'd decided to invite. And I said that of course I knew since, duh, I *helped* you decide, but I couldn't possibly tell and they'd have to wait like everyone else. And I love it! Do you love it? I mean, you've got to be the absolute most popular girl in school!"

As one cute ninth-grade guy—Randy Weaver, whose broad shoulders made him a shoo-in for the high-school football team next year—held her homeroom door open for her, Kat knew that Zoe was right. She, Kat Connors, was without a doubt the most popular girl in school. And she didn't mind it, not one bit.

. . .

At 2:58 p.m., all eyes were on the clock above the head of Mrs. Pittsenbarger, the social studies teacher. No one was paying her the least bit of attention. Everyone had pink on the brain. Especially Kat, who was counting down the seconds until the final bell rang.

As the last few minutes passed with the speed of molasses on an iceberg, Kat stole a glance over to Jules in the back of the classroom. They'd hardly spoken all day, although Kat hadn't made much of an effort. They had eaten lunch together, but Kat had been so swamped by girls who were stopping by the table to say hi that there wasn't much time to chat. When Araceli Chavez stopped by the table to give Kat the extra brownie her mom "accidentally" packed in her lunch, Kat saw Jules roll her eyes. She was sure that confirmed Jules's total lack of interest in the whole Glitter Girl scene.

But now, as the moment of the ticket giveaway approached, Kat wasn't so sure. Because now, as the last few seconds ticked away and she glanced over to Jules, she thought that she might have seen a hopeful, longing look in her friend's eyes. (Like that time in fifth grade when

Jules found that stray Maltese and really, really wanted to keep it.) Just then Jules quickly looked down, pretending to write something in her notebook, and suddenly Kat wasn't so sure again.

RING! As the three o'clock bell rang, the madness began. Kat hightailed it out the door without even the slightest glance back at Jules. So she missed the crestfallen look on her friend's face.

Kat made her way out of the classroom, and flanked by Darcy and Zoe, she pulled out the pink tickets and began passing them out whenever she saw someone on her list.

"Aly Washington!"

Screams.

"Hannah Stafford!"

More screams.

"Misty! Misty Wilkins," she called to Misty through the crowd. Misty lit up as she reached over a bunch of heads and took the coveted ticket.

"Where's Lily Diaz?" Kat asked and heard a squeal as she saw the top of Lily's head bob up and down over the crowd. As Kat reached past a group of girls to hand Lily her ticket, she saw the utter disappointment in the eyes of the "unchosen."

But she ignored it as best she could and continued

passing out the tickets as Darcy checked off the names on her list and Zoe acted as bodyguard, protecting Kat from anyone who was getting too close. "Daphne Momsette. Cee Cee Lewis." And so it went, name after name, squeal after squeal, the occasional "aw" of disappointment and even some sobs. But by now Kat had stopped noticing. She was too caught up in the excitement of the moment and this exhilarating feeling of, well, power that surged through her.

Finally Zoe turned to her and whispered, "That's it, except for Kelsey Miller. She had cheerleading practice right after school. She'll be in the gym."

Kat then held up a hand and was amazed and pretty darned thrilled that this tiny gesture caused instant silence. "That's it, ladies. Congrats to those of you who have been chosen. I'll see you Saturday night!"

So off she went, led by Zoe and Darcy toward the gym, leaving a sea of heartbreak and disappointment in their wake.

"OMG! Did you see Candace Mack?" laughed Zoe.

"I know, she was actually sobbing!" said Darcy.

"She was sobbing? Candace Mack?" asked Kat a little surprised. "Seriously?"

"I know! I mean, how could she even think we'd consider her? Puny little seventh grader," said Zoe as the trio pushed into the gym.

Kat started to feel a little guilty, but her guilt was interrupted by a feeling far more powerful when you're fourteen—the thrill of seeing your crush. As they entered the gym on their hunt for Kelsey, Kat's eyes caught those of Kyle, who was busy showing Coach Scofield his stuff during a pickup basketball game with some of the other ninth-grade boys.

"I don't see her," said Zoe scanning the gym.

"Maybe she's in the locker room," said Darcy.

"You guys check it out. I'll wait here," said Kat, not taking her eyes off Kyle. Darcy and Zoe headed back to the girls' locker room. Coach Scofield blew his whistle and told the boys to get a drink of water. Kat watched as Kyle walked past the water fountain and straight across the court toward her. Her heart caught in her throat as she took a couple of steps toward him and smiled.

"Nice job out there," Kat said, giggling a little and trying to think of something at least moderately intelligent to say about basketball. The best she could come up with was, "You're really good."

"Yeah? Thanks. Coach is going to announce the fall tournament team soon, so I want to be ready. What did *you* think, dork?" Kyle looked to Kat's left.

"Pretty good, pea brain. You might actually have a

shot," replied Jules. She had been sitting on the bleachers and Kat, with all her distractions, hadn't even seen her.

"Oh, hey, what are you doing here?" asked Kat, taken aback.

"Waiting for Kyle to finish practice so we can go home. What are *you* doing here?" asked Jules, her eye on the single pink ticket in Kat's hand.

Kat looked from Jules to Kyle, who was looking back at her with his dark piercing eyes.

"I'm, uh, I came to give out the last ticket to, uh…to you! I mean, if you want it. You don't have to if—" but Kat was cut off because Jules, in spite of herself, jumped up and gave her a *huge* hug that frankly shocked the heck out of Kat.

"I'd *love* to go!" said Jules, quickly composing herself. "I mean, you know, only if you really want me to come. I mean, it's not a big deal, whatever."

"Really? Cuz if you don't—" started Kat, backpedaling a little. But before she could go on…

"Kat Connors! Are you passing out those tickets on school grounds?"

Kat turned to see Ms. Donovan coming at her like a freight train. The crowd of boys around the drinking fountain simultaneously looked around to find the source of the commotion, and all eyes turned, for the second time today, to Kat.

"Uh, I thought it was okay as long as it was after school," offered Kat.

"No. It is *not* okay. Do you know that I passed at least a half dozen girls in tears in the hallway? Tears! This is exactly what I—"

"Hey! There a problem here?" asked Coach Scofield, who had crossed the gym to join them.

"C–coach Scofield!" said Ms. Donovan, whirling around and realizing for the first time that she was now within inches of her own crush. Kat could see that Ms. D was trying to play it cool. Well, for her, anyway. "No, there's n–no problem," the teacher stammered, playing with her glasses nervously. "It's just—just teenage girls, you know, being teenage girls. It's, uh, adolescents trying to establish parameters for their own social cohorts. It's all very Goneril and Cordelia from Act I of *Lear*."

"Uh, ma'am, I'm sorry. You lost me at adolescents," said the dumbfounded coach, not used to hearing so many syllables uttered at once that didn't involve the zone defense.

"Everything's cool, Coach." Kat jumped in, seeing that Ms. Donovan could use a lifeline before she turned completely into girl-nerd crush goo. "Coach Scofield, do you know Ms. Donovan? She's like a humongous supporter of the basketball program."

"Is that so?" said Coach Scofield, happy to have the conversation turn back to a topic that he knew something about: himself.

Ms. Donovan stood frozen in surprise, so Kat continued.

"Oh yeah," Kat continued. "She's totally about students being well-rounded. In fact, she was just saying how she's sure you'll be putting together a winning team this year and that we should all be at the games to cheer you on."

"Well, that's mighty nice of you, Ms. Donovan." He gave Ms. Donovan a smile that would light up a scoreboard. "I hope to see you at the games too, and I hope my boys don't disappoint this year."

"Rachel. Call me Rachel." Ms. Donovan smiled, momentarily forgetting entirely about the shattered pubescent egos strewn around the hallways of Willkie at that very moment.

While Donovan and Scofield started to play another round of Middle-Aged Mystery Date, Kat turned to Jules and said with a self-satisfied grin, "Spider-Man strikes again!"

Her smile quickly faded when she spotted Darcy and Zoe emerging from the girls' locker room with a very excited Kelsey in tow. And Kat, without a single ticket left to give, decided there was only one way to handle it.

"Gotta go!" said Kat as she quickly flung her backpack over her shoulder.

"Hey, Kat! Wanna go for burgers sometime?" Kyle called after her.

"Really? I would love to! Call me!" she said with a delighted smile before quickly ducking out the nearest exit, much to Zoe, Darcy, and Kelsey's confusion.

Jules looked amazed and horrified at what she had just witnessed. She didn't know what was worse. Her brother asking Kat for a date. Ew. Or Ms. Donovan and Coach Scofield. Seriously?

Then again, she, Jules, displayed some fairly pathetic behavior herself when Kat had finally given her the invitation. She hated herself for how much she wanted to be invited. And how desperate she had felt the whole day, agonizing over it like all those silly girls at school. She told herself she only wanted to be invited because she was Kat's best friend, and best friends never leave each other out of anything.

But as she turned over the pink invitation in her hand and the rhinestones glimmered in the lights of the gym, she had to admit that it did feel good, being one of the chosen ones for a change. She wanted to believe it so badly she didn't even let herself think about the fact that Kat, who said she had come to the gym to give her the ticket, had no idea Jules was even going to be there.

Chapter 8

For Now Sits Expectation in the Air

At 9 a.m. Saturday morning, a brown delivery truck pulled up to Kat's house on Jasmine Court. Kat dashed to the window and watched as the driver struggled to pull the huge box off the truck and onto a dolly. The wheels of the dolly went *click, click, click* over the sidewalk and seemed to be straining from the weight of the box. The thing was as big as one of those mini European cars that get such good gas mileage that Jules was always rambling on about. Kat's mother signed for the box and tipped the driver for wrestling that behemoth into the living room. Kat looked from her mom to the box and took a deep breath. Whew!

Across the cul-de-sac, Jules was still in bed. She had stayed up the night before trying to concentrate on the sonnets for the Shakespeare Club. She was supposed to recite one at the meeting next week and they had to pick another one for the Renaissance Faire, but she couldn't decide which one.

She looked from her thick book of poems on the floor

to the pink invitation on her desk. The more she thought about the party, the more nervous she became. Which was silly. She'd slept over at Kat's a million times. But still. Darcy? And Zoe? Really? And a bunch of girls who she didn't even know, and even if she did know them, they seemed mean and silly and superficial and a whole bunch of other not-too-flattering adjectives that she'd just as soon keep to herself, thank you very much. The grinding of the gears of the delivery truck had caught her attention, so when she pulled back her blinds and peeked out the window, she caught a glimpse of the box as it was being wheeled into the Connors' house. Man, it was so *big*!

At that exact moment, five blocks away, Nickelodeon's Saturday lineup blared from the TV in Darcy's room. Zoe thought she was a baby for still watching that channel when there were much cooler, more "grown-up" shows on other networks, shows where beautiful teenagers hooked up with other beautiful teenagers while their parents vacationed in the Hamptons, wherever that was. Darcy didn't care. She liked Nickelodeon.

Let Zoe say whatever she wanted. Zoe didn't know everything. But she *did* know Kat Connors, and that made it worth tolerating all of Zoe's stuck-up opinions and criticisms. Because if there was one thing Darcy liked more than Nickelodeon, it was being popular. And she absolutely, positively couldn't wait for Kat's super-cool slumber party that evening. In fact, thinking of it distracted Darcy from her TV show and she totally missed seeing her favorite actress get slimed. Bummer!

Just as green slime dripped down the actress's face, the brown delivery truck sped past Darcy's house, having dropped off its precious cargo at the Connors residence. The truck turned round the corner and moved two blocks up Waveland Way, past a house where Zoe sat motionless on a piano bench and watched as a stopwatch in her hand ticked off seconds. Only twenty-seven minutes to go. She usually practiced for about three minutes so that the sound of music would be in the air in the house, but she knew her parents demanded she put in a half an hour every day, so she usually just sat on the bench for that time and daydreamed.

She had been quite a little player when she was ten years old, but she hadn't been progressing much lately. *Who cares*, she thought. Stars don't play the piano anyway. Little shy kids like Teresa Watanabe from next door play piano, while girls like Zoe were in the spotlight. Zoe's mom walked by and sighed. Two hundred dollars a month for lessons, and for what? For her daughter to sit on a piano bench and daydream about some silly slumber party.

Outside the house, a group of teenagers jogged by. It was the ninth-grade Willkie athletes on their Saturday workout. Driving along and keeping pace in his blue Corolla was Coach Scofield. Kyle led the group of runners. He usually did. He was the best-conditioned athlete of the bunch, or so Coach Scofield said after the last practice. They were going to announce the fall tournament team soon, and Kyle couldn't let up if he was going to make it.

He looked back to see if Scofield was noticing him and saw Jaden Atkins, the sweet-shooting point guard, sucking wind a half block behind him. *Hey, Jaden, maybe you oughta build some low-cost housing for the poor sometime. It does wonders for your endurance!* As Kyle kicked into another gear and started his sprint back to the school, his thoughts turned to Kat, which had been happening a lot lately.

They turned on Waveland and ran past Dance Revolution, down from the Wendy's in the strip mall, where a pack of young mothers stood outside and sipped lattes while their three-year-olds pretended they were ballerinas behind the huge picture windows of the studio. In the next room, Ms. Donovan sat behind the receptionist's desk where she worked every Saturday for a little extra money. She absentmindedly twirled a pencil in her fingers and stared past the mothers outside.

She could see the group of teenage boys wearing blue and gold and running in the distance. Wolves colors. She knew they were Willkie boys, probably Coach Scofield's. She quickly perked up when she spotted Scofield hanging out the window of his pace car. She watched as he suddenly put on the brakes and stared past the boys at something. She followed his gaze and saw he was gawking at an attractive young woman with blond highlights coming out of the beauty salon across the way. As he drove off, Ms. Donovan glanced over at the beauty salon. Maybe the Connors girl was right—maybe some highlights and contacts weren't such a bad idea, after all.

Down from Dance Revolution, in the drive-thru of the Wendy's, Kelsey Miller was still pouting in the back of her mom's minivan. How could Zoe and Darcy have said that she was invited when she wasn't? What kind of cruel trick was that, anyway? Was that little airhead Kat Connors behind it all? Let her have her little slumber party. Who wants to go to such a stupid thing? Besides, supposedly her parents were getting a divorce. Kelsey took her Wendy's apple pecan salad from her mom in the front seat. She didn't feel like eating it.

The minivan headed down the street past the Marriott Inn, where at that exact moment in Room 211, Chelsea

Ambrose was putting on an earring and talking into her Bluetooth headset at the same time. "Yeah, Amy," she said, "I just confirmed the shipment. Where are we with that girl in Houston? Who do we have there? Melanie? Have her tell the mom that we could go another way. I don't care about that. Not every girl has what it takes to be a Glitter Girl. Just take care of it."

Chelsea hung up. She looked at herself critically in the mirror. She removed a silk scarf from around her neck and tossed it on the bed. The scarf caught the air like a parachute and floated down, landing softly on top of an advance copy of next month's *Seventeen* magazine. The smiling face of teen singing sensation Jessica Aguirre and her perfect teeth were on the cover. In the corner of the magazine cover was Chelsea's biggest success yet. A splashy headline read, "Are *YOU* Glitter Girl material? Take our super quiz inside!" Chelsea's hard work was finally starting to pay off. The thirty-fifth floor had never seemed closer.

Next to the hotel was the massive White Oak Mall. At that very moment on the third level, across from the food court at Forever 21, Aly Washington and Misty Wilkins explained to their mothers *again* why they simply couldn't go to this sleepover in *old* pajamas. It wasn't going to happen. Misty's mom clicked a few numbers into a little calculator in her pocketbook, and looked at the pink cami and plaid short shorts number Misty was showing off for Aly and absolutely *loved*. Mrs. Wilkins shrugged in the salesgirl's general direction and handed her a credit card. The gas bill could wait until payday, she supposed.

In the parking lot across the street, Kat pushed a shopping cart toward the gourmet grocery store at the corner of Benning Parkway and Memorial Drive. Kat's mom insisted on picking up a few things for the party, even though Chelsea said her company would be footing the bill and she would be coming by with what she called some "special treats" for everyone later that evening. Chelsea was so cool. She'd been so nice to Kat's mom too, even when her mom was freaking out about whether or not the box would arrive on time and the party would come off without a hitch.

Sometimes, it almost seemed like her mom wanted this more than she did. But then again, Kat *did* think it was pretty cool. All the posts on her blog had been so positive in the last week, and the traffic was *way* up. Everyone online was just dying to know what kind of treasures would be in the Glitter Girl box once it was opened. Kat had promised her readers she'd "live blog" the party as much as she could, and her reviews would all be online by the next Monday. Imagine. So many girls looking to *her*, the same way that maybe she looked to Chelsea. It was kinda cool.

The automatic doors of the supermarket opened, and Kat followed her mom toward the fancy pastry counter.

The party would start in eight hours.

Chapter 9

Canst Thou Bring Me to the Party?

A pair of white denim capris. Sandals. And a printed bib tank top she'd bought with the gift certificate from the Gap that her grandma had given her on her last birthday.

Jules looked at herself in the mirror of her bedroom and made a face as if she'd just sucked on a lemon. It wasn't much, this outfit, but then again there wasn't much in her closet in the first place. She had her standard rotation of T-shirts promoting various causes, and two or three pairs of boot-cut jeans she wore to school most days. Before tonight, she'd spent about twelve seconds on the daily chore of choosing what to wear, and that was on a good day. But tonight, with "them" invited to the party as well, she felt like she had to make at least an effort to look like someone with a sense of style.

Still not all that thrilled with what she had on, Jules looked out her window to the Connors's house. How many girls were there already? She had seen at least twelve girls arrive so far, plus Chelsea, but she couldn't be sure. Zoe had come in looking like she thought she was all that, looking way more than thirteen years old; God knows what kind of stunt she had to pull to get her parents to buy *that* outfit.

Oh forget it, Jules thought, *let's just get this over with*. She grabbed her backpack and sleeping bag and started down the stairs.

"Who died?" came a voice from the living room. *Oh geez. Kyle. Great.*

"What are you talking about, jock boy?" said Jules reflexively, still not exactly sure where he was.

"Those clothes," said Kyle's disembodied voice. "Either you're heading for a funeral, or your buddy Al Gore is in town."

By this time, Jules had made it to the bottom of the stairs and encountered her brother sprawled out flat on his back on the living-room floor. He held a basketball over his head and flicked it high into the air with his right hand, and then did the same with his left, critically examining the spin on the ball and the position of his hand after each shot. Again and again the ball flew high in the air, almost hitting the ceiling fan, and then it came down, submitting to the laws of gravity and landing back in Kyle's oversized teenage hands.

"What in the name of LeBron James are you doing?"

she said, mentioning the only basketball player that she'd ever heard of.

"The ball is supposed to land on my hand exactly in the same spot I shot it from," Kyle said seriously, letting the ball fly again. "That tells me my form is on track. So I answered your question, you answer mine. What's the deal with the getup? Hot date in Nerdland?"

"Ha, ha. No, for your information, brainless, tonight is that Glitter Girl sleepover thing at Kat's house. You remember, I was talking to Mom about it last night at dinner."

Kyle paused a moment with the ball in his hands when he heard Kat's name. Then he sent it back into the air. "Oh that. To be honest, I don't pay a whole lot of attention most of the time when you're talking."

"Do I use words that are too big for your little pea brain, jockoid?" Jules said, knocking the ball out of her brother's hand as she headed for the door.

Slam!

"Say hi to Kat!" he yelled after her, even though she was halfway down the driveway. Kyle retrieved the ball, which had ended up under the coffee table, and threw it into the air once again.

"Swish!" he whispered to himself.

• • •

The early October sky was starting to darken as Jules made her way across the cul-de-sac. She stopped for a moment to pull her little neighbor Justina Halperin's tricycle out of the street. Since the Halperins moved in last year, Justina was always leaving her stuff everywhere, but Jules and Kat had been keeping an eye on her. The last thing they needed in the cul-de-sac was some disagreement when one of the neighbors ran over that trike backing out of his garage. Also, moving it bought Jules a few moments, allowing her to delay the inevitable.

Having safely deposited the tricycle and without further distractions or excuses, Jules continued down the sidewalk and opened the gate that led to the Connors's front door. She rang the bell and took a deep breath.

Instead of seeing Kat's smiling face, or even that of her mom answering the door, she looked up to see none other than Chelsea Ambrose.

"Oh," said Chelsea, looking back inside the house and closing the door behind her. "Maybe you didn't know. Kat's a little busy tonight. She's hosting an event that's sort of 'invite only.' Sorry." She began to close the door.

Jules felt a primordial shiver going up her spine. Just like she'd heard about in biology class. Classic fight-or-flight reaction.

"Uh, yeah," she said, choosing the former and stopping the door before Chelsea could close it. "That's kind of what I'm here for."

She produced the glittery pink invitation from her back-pack, held it out defiantly for Chelsea to see, and marched past her into the house.

She smiled slyly as she entered the foyer. *Round one to Jules*, she thought to herself.

Jules walked into Kat's house and looked around. Trudy, no doubt under the watchful eye of Chelsea, had simply *transformed* the place. In one corner of the living room was one of those cool karaoke machines that had its own screen so you could film a video of yourself singing and then play it back right away.

A few of the girls were playing Blind Man's Karaoke, a game Kat and Jules had invented a couple of sleepovers ago. They put the CD on "random play" and blindfolded one girl. She had to recognize the song and sing along without making a mistake. Once she blew a line, her time was up and the next girl could try. At the moment, Daphne Momsette was bellowing out something that sounded vaguely like Jessica Aguirre's latest hit, "What's It Gonna Be, Boy?" and had made it through the first verse and half the chorus before she flubbed up.

"Twenty-nine seconds!" yelled out Cee Cee Lewis, the official timer. "Good, but not good enough! Who's next?"

Next to the karaoke corner was a table full of snacks, where Darcy and Zoe were busy dipping carrot sticks into ranch dressing.

"These are soo good. I could eat them *all* right now!" exclaimed Zoe, closing her eyes and letting the flavor of the ranch dressing melt in her mouth before she swallowed.

"Yeah, the only thing missing is the ketchup!" Darcy said, as if *everybody* ate their carrot sticks smothered in ketchup.

By this time, Chelsea had caught up with Jules again and grabbed her by the shoulder. A little *too* firmly for Jules's taste, it might be added.

"Come on, sweetie," said Chelsea in perhaps the unsweetest way possible. "Let's go find Kat."

Chelsea led Jules out through the sliding door to the backyard, where a few of the girls sat on deck chairs around Kat's swimming pool and drank some kind of frozen concoction Kat's mom had created out of Hawaiian Punch and 7UP. Mrs. Connors served the drinks in tall glasses with the obligatory umbrellas sticking out of them. She made the rounds while the girls sat by the pool and tried to imagine how starlets in Hollywood would act if they were sitting around a pool.

Kat was sitting on the edge of the pool with her feet in the water, talking to a girl Jules didn't recognize. Kat said something to her and the girl laughed loudly. *That's Kat*, thought Jules. *She makes everyone feel better about being around her.* It was a gift from the girl gods.

"Kat!" said Chelsea with Jules in tow. "Look what I found!"

Jules looked severely at Chelsea. That did *not* sound good coming from her.

"Jules!" said Kat, enthusiastically coming up to her with her arm around the new girl. "Have you met Angie Ferris? She's just transferred from Boyton Middle School. She's in my second-period computer class."

Kat and Angie looked at each other smiling and simultaneously burst out, "Windows for Blonds!" as if it were the funniest thing *ever*. "Isn't that cool?" Kat continued.

"Uh," said Jules, not nearly as comfortable with new people as Kat was, "I guess."

"We were just saying that we hoped you didn't get lost!" said Mrs. Connors, coming over to Jules with a tray of drinks in her hand and offering her one.

"Angie," said Chelsea, pulling her away from Kat's grasp a bit, "why don't you show Jules where the other girls are putting their things?"

"I could do tha—" said Kat.

"That's okay," said Chelsea, cutting her off sweetly. "This will give Jules and Angie a chance to talk."

"Uh, okay," said Angie obediently. "Come on." She took Jules and the two made their way back into the house.

As they walked into the living room, they passed the huge box that Jules had seen the brown truck deliver earlier in the day. Since its arrival, it had been decorated with colorful wrapping-paper designs, and a gigantic lace ribbon that now smiled at passersby from the top of the box. Above the box, suspended from the ceiling, was an enormous digital clock that looked like a frilly pink version of one of those Countdown Clocks the bad guys were always using to blow up the world in the spy movies from the 1960s that Jules liked to watch with her dad.

But this clock was counting down to something far cooler than the end of the world and the destruction of every living organism on the planet. This clock was one of fifty perfectly synchronized clocks, all designed to read "00:00:00" at precisely 9 p.m. Eastern Standard Time, when all the Glitter Girls from around the country would simultaneously experience Glitter Girl products for the first time. It was another of Chelsea Ambrose's little touches that had impressed the Board of Directors at Remoulet headquarters. The clock now read thirty-seven minutes to go. A few girls crowded around the box and watched the numbers on the Glitter Girl clock tick down. They giggled in anticipation.

Angie pulled Jules away from the clock and up the stairs toward the bedroom.

"Come on," she said. "I'll show you where the bedroom is."

Jules could hardly believe what she was hearing. A few months ago, this girl hadn't even known Kat and was going to some school on the other side of town, but now she was giving *her* a tour of Kat's house? It would be laughable if it weren't so weird. Jules knew it wasn't Angie's fault, so she dutifully played along as Angie pointed out things Jules had known about since she was in diapers.

Meanwhile in the backyard, Chelsea had cornered Kat by the Connors's wet bar near the pool.

"Kat," said Chelsea, still cool as a cucumber, "I don't remember seeing this girl Jules on the list of names you gave me."

"Oh that. Yeah, I meant to tell you," Kat lied. "Kelsey Miller couldn't make it so I asked Jules to step in at the last minute so we would still have twenty girls."

Chelsea studied Kat carefully, not sure if she was telling the truth or if she was as effortless a liar as she was herself.

"Well, that's fine. It's no problem for me," Chelsea said, throwing in a whopper of her own. "I just hope she'll feel comfortable around the other girls. She's just, you know, *not* like them."

Kat knew exactly what Chelsea meant but defended her friend anyway. "No," she said, "Jules is cool. It just takes her a while to get comfortable at parties. I'm sure she'll be fine."

"Are you sure?"

"If I'm lyin', I'm dyin'," Kat said, smiling sweetly at Chelsea.

"You have no idea," said Chelsea in a way that, despite the sweet smile she flashed back at Kat, left Kat totally unnerved.

Chapter 10

We Few, We Happy Few

"Ten! Nine! Eight! Seven! Six! Five! Four! Three! Two! One!"

Like on New Year's Eve in Times Square in New York City, the girls counted down along with the Glitter Girl clock as it made its way backward to 00:00:00. Then suddenly what seemed like a thousand little hands descended on the huge box and began ripping it apart. The ripping was so ferocious that it was hard to believe it came from dainty fourteen-year-old fingers painted in innocent pink, purple, and teal rather than a pack of jackals bringing down its prey. Those pretty little hands could do some serious damage, because within a minute the big box was totally gutted and dozens of smaller boxes were spilling out everywhere. It was like a mamma box had given birth to a giant litter of baby boxes!

Before you knew it, all those "baby" boxes were mercilessly ripped open and their contents revealed. Contents such as bedazzled hair accessories, shimmery eye makeup, body glitter, solar-powered key chains that flashed your name, rhinestone-encrusted flip-flops, super-cool sunglasses with mirrored lenses, leopard-print throw pillows with a secret compartment for a diary, and tankini swimsuits covered in the cutest little cherry print ever. Then of course there was a whole line of accessories from T-shirts to notebooks and pens that sported the words "Study? I'm Here to See My Friends" and nail polish that actually changed color depending on your mood!

And that wasn't even the coolest stuff. There was software that let you design your own line of clothing and then stage a totally fabulous virtual fashion show to the music of your choice (downloaded for a small fee, of course). There were MP3 players with an app that could figure out the star charts of you and up to five of your BFFs and then calculate the next ten years of your daily horoscope! There were flash drives in every animal print imaginable, as well as fuzzy slippers with a recordable chip that you could make say things like, "It's too early. Wake me when it's noon," or, "Step aside. Fabulous coming through," whenever you took a step.

Kat looked around at it all and proclaimed at the top of her lungs, "This is the most therocious night ever!" The girls all cheered.

. . .

Two hours later, the house looked like the aftermath of the most decadent Christmas morning ever. The girls, now in their pj's, sat amid a mountain of discarded packaging. Tufts of hot pink, white, and black marabou floated through the air like puffy snowflakes as the girls excitedly tried everything in sight.

"Cool! Awesome! Sweet!" were some of the words still heard as the girls tried out various items, sometimes even getting into a tug-of-war over them.

Kat sat cross-legged on the floor near the fireplace with her laptop across her knees. She'd promised her readers she would live blog the whole night, and she typed a mile a minute as the other girls pranced around in their new Glitter Gear. She was positively beaming over this stuff.

Guess what?

she wrote,

I feel confident that the forecast for this fall is sunny and warm, with a definite chance of glitter and a "cool" front moving in!

She loved weather analogies.

Chelsea Ambrose, who had been peeking over Kat's shoulder as she typed, walked around the room, surveying the frilly chaos she had created.

A feeding frenzy, Chelsea thought as she watched it all with a self-satisfied smirk. She scanned the room and noted the hungry look in the eyes of this pack of girls. The look from which big sales are made. It was the look that they all had. All of them except…that Jules girl. Chelsea's smirk faded.

Jules sat at the center island eating off a picked-over snack tray, observing the madness from afar, not even tempted to pick up a single Glitter Girl item. It irked Chelsea. Who did this girl think she was, sitting there high up on her bar stool like she was above all this?

"Is there a problem?" asked Chelsea, sidling up next to Jules.

Not sure she was being spoken to, Jules looked up, surprised, dropping a glob of guacamole from her chip onto her white capris. But Chelsea was indeed looking straight at her.

"No," said Jules, trying to wipe the guacamole off her pants and only making it worse.

"Then come and join the fun," said Chelsea in a voice that was more threatening than inviting.

"No thanks. I–I'm not really into this kind of stuff," said Jules as she wiped up the mess she'd made on herself.

"You're not into 'this kind of stuff'?" Chelsea repeated quite loudly, sounding offended.

Suddenly the room went quiet as Jules realized that all eyes had turned to her. That included Kat, who had been blogging about the makeover Aly Washington was doing on Misty Wilkins using a triple palette of blue eye shadows (cerulean, cornflower, and a shade called mouthwash). Kat was having such a good time capturing the moment that she had forgotten all about Jules.

"Well, I'm sorry you find this all soooo boring," said Chelsea pointedly.

There were a few snickers from around the room. Zoe sniffed haughtily and gave Kat an "I told you so" look. Kat didn't like where this was heading. She quickly set down her laptop and jumped in.

"Here, Jules. Try out this eye shadow Aly's using. It would look so good with your skin tone," offered Kat, holding out the little container.

Unlike Kat, Jules was always on the verge of humiliation when she was the center of attention. She was already feeling really out of place at this ridiculous party. She wouldn't know what to do with three shades of eye shadow if her life depended on it. And now the whole room would know. So instead of admitting her true feelings, she relied on her usual defense mechanism, sarcasm.

"Yeah, maybe if I was a Smurf or one of the Na'vi on the planet Pandora," she replied.

Tittering and whispers could be heard around the room. Even a barely audible "lame" that Kat was sure came from Zoe. Kat cringed in embarrassment. How could Jules do this to her? In front of Chelsea? When she knew how badly Kat wanted to be the Face of Glitter Girl!

"There's other stuff here I'm sure you'll like," said Kat, trying to salvage the moment.

"Yes, Jules. Surely there's something here that would be interesting—even to a girl like you," said Chelsea. More snickers from around the room.

A girl like you? This is exactly what Jules had been worried about. Not fitting in. And she was mad now that these stupid girls were laughing at her. And mad at herself that she had ever even wanted to come to this stupid party to begin with.

"I doubt it," she said, digging in her heels.

"Oh you'll like this!" offered Darcy from the corner. As usual, she was completely oblivious to the tension that now filled the room. "It's so cool. Look, it's shaped like a pretty, little pink daisy pin but like, it's secretly a camera!"

Desperate to end the weirdness, Kat rushed over to Darcy and grabbed the pin, making a huge point to gush about it. "What? That's amazing! How does it work, Chelsea?"

Temporarily forgetting Jules, Chelsea came over and proudly explained, "Oh, this is fabulous. It's called a Slam Cam. It's a tiny covert video camera specifically for spying."

"Ooooh!" went about eight of the girls simultaneously at the word "spying."

Chelsea smiled and continued, "You can catch your friends and family in funny situations and post the videos on the Internet. Or let's say you and your friend are having an argument. You can secretly record it, and later when your friend denies saying something, which, let's admit, they *always* do…you just pop out the drive, put it in your computer, and bingo! She's busted!"

There were more "oohs" and "ahhs" around the room. Zoe proclaimed she absolutely *had* to have one. But then…

"That sounds creepy. Not to mention illegal."

Kat turned. She couldn't believe it! Jules just refused to shut up!

"My mom's a—" Jules began.

"Yeah, we know. Your mom's a lawyer. But not everything's a major crime. Some things are just fun," said Kat.

Jules was a little stung by her friend accusing her of not seeing the fun in things. But not all things were funny. Not to her. Suddenly she felt very defensive.

"Oh, come on. You have to admit...*this* is a major crime!" said Jules. She picked up an engineer's cap from a pile of Glitter Gear. It was pink-and-white plaid with rhinestones all around the band.

"Excuse me. But I'll have you know that our market research shows this hat will be the hottest next trend in teen wardrobe accessories," said Chelsea.

"Well, as an actual teen, I can tell you it's lame," said Jules. "Ask Kat. She'll tell you the same thing."

Smiling, Jules looked at Kat, knowing full well that Kat did not do hats. Not ever, under any circumstances, nuh-uh. This Chelsea chick was in for a rude awakening.

"Kat?" Chelsea held the engineer's cap out to Kat to put on, daring her really.

Now all eyes were on Kat. She could not believe Jules, putting her on the spot like this. Knowing full well how she felt about hats.

Kat took the hat from Chelsea, hemmed and hawed a bit, and held it out in front of her as if it were one of her little cousin's dirty diapers. "It, uh, it's pretty sweet," said Kat finally. And to Jules's amazement, Kat put on the hat.

Kat! Who had never, not once, not in all the years Jules had known her, ever put on a hat.

Not even that one time at the new Aquatic Center for Ellie Boyle's fifth birthday party when it was like a hundred degrees. Her mom had said she had to wear a hat or she couldn't be in the sun, but Kat wouldn't budge. She sat underneath the picnic table the entire time and even sang "Happy Birthday" and ate her cake from under there, just to avoid wearing a silly birthday hat.

And now Kat was wearing a hat. She was, well, Kat in a hat! Chelsea gave Jules a pretty snotty look as looks go. Jules thought she would barf.

Jules looked around at the girls, most of them snickering at her. Except of course Darcy, who was on Kat's laptop trying to use the design program and failing miserably. She saw Zoe, who was staring at her guacamole-stained capris, whisper something to Misty, and they both cracked up.

Angry and upset, Jules grabbed her sleeping bag and headed to the front door.

"Jules! Wait. Where are you going?" asked Kat. Even if she was ticked at Jules, she didn't want her to leave.

"Home."

"Don't forget your goodie bag, sweetie." Chelsea shoved

a bag in her hand and Jules could have sworn Chelsea was nudging her out the door.

Jules ran out of the living room. Kat hesitated a second and then went after her.

Kat caught up to Jules on the front porch of the house.

"Hey, stop. Don't be that way," said Kat.

"What way? You mean be myself unlike some people I know?" Jules looked at the stupid hat Kat was still wearing.

Self-conscious, Kat pulled it off. "I'm just having fun. What's wrong with that?"

"If being a sell-out is your idea of fun, I don't want any part of it." Jules stormed off.

Kat looked back into the house to see the rest of the partygoers crowding at the front window, watching the whole thing. She saw that Chelsea was watching too, looking her up and down. How much had she seen of that mess? Kat wondered if Chelsea was at that very moment striking her off the list of candidates to be the Face of Glitter Girl. Kat was angry at Jules for embarrassing her like this. She took a deep breath and stepped back into the house.

"I am sooo sorry for that whole scene," said Kat, completely red-faced.

"I told you not to invite her," said Zoe.

"I guess I should have left her off the list like we had

planned in the first place," Kat admitted, desperate to make things right in Chelsea's eyes.

"Then why *did* you invite her?" asked Chelsea in a penetrating way that made Kat feel like she'd better come up with a very good answer or else she was definitely not going to be the Face of Glitter Girl.

"Well, I don't know, I—uh—her brother was standing there—"

"Her brother *is* really cute," added Zoe and several girls nodded, which empowered Kat and made her feel she was on the right track.

"Yeah. And I felt guilty. And, and I guess, I guess it was like a, you know, a pity invite!" said Kat.

There were murmurs of understanding from some of the girls. But it was Chelsea's reaction that concerned Kat.

Chelsea broke into a smile. She went over to Kat and put her arm around her.

"You have a good heart, sweetie, but you'll have to learn that in life, heart will only get you so far. Not everyone is Glitter Girl material. Now. Who wants some free lip gloss?"

The girls cheered and as they all started back to the family room, bubbly and talking and laughing, Kat was relieved the party was back on track. Still, she felt a pang of guilt deep inside and took a quick glance out the big picture window where she could see the light go on in Jules's room. When Kat finally rejoined her friends at the party, that guilt made it hard for her to appreciate the OMG! prettiest shade of gloss she had ever laid eyes on.

Chapter 11

Kat's Influence:
Like a Wreath of Radiant Fire

By midnight, Chelsea had gone back to her hotel and the party had become pretty much like every other slumber party—a few girls got sleepy and flopped on the sofa in front of the TV, where they were streaming a movie everybody had already seen a hundred times. A few others were gossiping about boys in the kitchen while they ate some leftover raw cookie dough that never quite made it into the oven. Some others were still sorting through the box of goodies from Glitter Girl, making sure they hadn't missed any treasure in their first frenzied rush.

Up in her room, Kat Connors was sitting on her bed, typing away at her laptop, updating her blog with some last-minute additions she hadn't been able to do during the party. She used her new Slam Cam to snap and upload some quick stills of the products from the box and was busy posting them to the blog with her comments on each one. Across the street, Jules's bedroom light had gone out a long time ago, and to be honest, while Kat had been a little bummed about what happened earlier, she decided not to give it a whole lot of thought. It was just Jules being Jules. Kat figured they'd be cool by the time school came around on Monday.

Before she left, Chelsea had given her some "ideas" for what other things to say on the blog about each product. Chelsea made it clear that Kat could write anything she wanted, but she also said there were certain things about the products that she wanted to make sure Kat "didn't forget" in all the excitement of the evening. Kat looked at the three pages of Chelsea's typed notes in front of her.

It was harmless enough stuff, she thought. Saying that one lip gloss was "sassy" or that the shades of nail polish were "everything a girl could ask for and more." No, they weren't *exactly* her thoughts about the products, but it *was* pretty cool stuff. Besides, she was tired. And when you're tired, somebody else's words just seem easier to type than thinking of nouns and verbs and adjectives all your own.

She even gave a positive review to that sparkly engineer's hat Jules had thought was so hideous. Well, Kat thought the same thing, to be honest, and not just because she didn't like hats—it truly was atrocious. But Chelsea had been *sooo* nice the whole evening and given them so much stuff. She closed her blog with the announcement that all this Glitter Girl stuff would be available exclusively at the White Oak Mall the next day (Chelsea had rented out an empty jewelry boutique for just that purpose) and that if customers would mention Kat's blog, they'd get 10 percent off all their purchases.

Kat read over the blog entry one last time. Her dad had always drilled it into her that her grammar and spelling should be impeccable, even on the Internet. It all looked good. She wrinkled her nose a bit when she read the part about the engineer's hat but didn't change anything. It was all more or less how she felt…sort of. She clicked on Post and voilà!—her words were part of the information super-highway. Kat turned off the laptop and looked at the clock. 1:47 a.m. Not bad for a sleepover. She put her head on her pillow, and before the clock hit 1:48, she was asleep.

● ● ●

Kat's mom once told her about a shampoo commercial from when Trudy was a teenager, where the girl on the commercial says she loved the shampoo so much she would "tell two friends" about it, and then those girls would tell two other friends who would tell two more friends, and so on and so on, until the entire TV screen was full of girls who were all in love with the same shampoo. Well, Kat's blog was kind of like that shampoo commercial.

By the time she and the other slumber-party girls woke up on Sunday morning for Trudy's waffles with strawberry butter, the entire city around them was simply abuzz about Glitter Girl. And this was not just Willkie girls. Girls of every age from every nook and cranny of the city had been reading and forwarding Kat's blog and pestering their parents and squirming through church and waiting impatiently for the White Oak Mall to open at 10 a.m.

By nine, the crowd outside the mall was two hundred strong, and there was more jockeying for position at the front of the line than you'd see at the Kentucky Derby. The security guards and mall managers scratched their heads. But the girls just kept coming. By nine thirty, the line wound around the parking lot, and a few local cops had been called off their regular shifts to run traffic control at the entrance. At ten, when the doors finally *did* open, the crowd flowed into the mall like a hunting party of lionesses with the scent of fresh zebra in the air.

Outside the temporary Glitter Girl store, a barely rested Chelsea Ambrose stood smiling from ear to ear, watching the girls rush by with their mothers in tow. She couldn't believe her good fortune. The sleepover had gone well to be sure, aside from that little issue with the frumpy neighbor girl, but this turnout exceeded even her own high expectations. Numbers coming in from the other states were solid, but these were off the charts! She had always known Kat Connors was a good choice, but *this*! This was lightning in a bottle.

By noon, the entire Glitter Girl store had sold out. Everything had been snapped up by girls eager to be the first to sport Glitter Gear at school the next day. Chelsea walked through the empty store as a few of the temporary employees cleaned up. The place looked like Whoville on Christmas morning after the Grinch had tossed everything in his sled and headed back up Mount Crumpit. There was nothing left but bare walls and wire. But unlike the Whos in Kat's favorite Dr. Seuss book, Chelsea was not about to join hands with anyone in the town square and sing. Instead, Chelsea had already started counting the money.

Kat, who had all the Glitter Girl stuff she needed at the moment, was one of the few girls in town who didn't make the pilgrimage to the White Oak Mall to shop for Glitter Gear. She went for an entirely different reason—Jules. Her birthday was coming up, and Kat hadn't gotten her present yet. And considering what had gone down the night before, Kat wanted to make sure it was an extra nice one.

As Kat walked through the mall, she was amazed at the madness that was happening at the temporary Glitter Girl shop. It certainly was clear that Glitter Girl was a hit, just like Chelsea had said it would be. The vague thought of giving Jules a Glitter Girl gift card as a gag gift crossed Kat's mind for a moment, but she quickly shook it off. Now was not the time for jokes, especially not about Glitter Girl. In fact, she made a point of steering clear of the mayhem at the Glitter Girl store completely, for fear of seeming over-eager to Chelsea.

Instead, Kat wandered through Forever 21 and Target and Macy's, but she couldn't really find anything that seemed to say "Jules." In fact, most of the stuff she saw practically screamed out "NOT JULES" instead. Kat decided to steer clear of the clothes, fashion, and beauty product sections of the other stores as well.

However, in the corner of the mall, there was a store Kat knew about, but just barely. The only reason it was on her radar was that it was on the way to that cart that sold cinnamon pretzels. It was a little store with a dingy sign: "McPhee & Sullivan, Independent Booksellers." It had been there as long as the mall existed but Kat had never set foot in the place.

Now, she entered the store. It wasn't like one of those well-lit, well-organized bookstores where Kat and her mom would go to buy a book for Kat's dad to read on the plane.

Instead, new and used books were piled to the ceiling in no particular order that Kat could decipher. An elderly man who looked a bit like Ebenezer Scrooge from *A Christmas Carol* sat on a stool behind the counter scribbling in a notebook. Kat nervously approached the ancient salesman.

"Excuse me," Kat said, barely audible.

No reaction. A little louder this time. "Excuse me."

The old man looked up at her, almost surprised to be seeing a customer, or at least a customer under the age of one hundred twelve.

"Well hello, young miss," the salesman said, with an accent that sounded a little English or Irish or Scottish or something. Kat could never tell the difference. "Would you be wanting a book today?"

"Uh, yeah, I think so," Kat replied. "I'm looking for a present for my friend. It's her birthday."

"Would she be around your age then?" the bookseller inquired, setting down his notebook and wiping his hands on a pea-green apron that must have been as old as he was.

"Uh, yeah, we're the same age," Kat replied. "I really want to give her something special. And she loves to read." Saying that, Kat remembered when she and Jules used to devour books and have reading contests during the summer to see who could read the most pages in a week. That hadn't happened in a while. In fact, Kat could barely remember the last book she had picked up because she *wanted* to read it.

"How about one of the Harry Potters?" suggested the old man. "They're still quite popular with the young people."

"I think she's got all of those."

"All righty then, could you give me a wee bit of a hint so I can steer us in the right direction?"

"Well, she's in the Shakespeare Club at school," Kat offered.

The old man's eyes lit up. "Shakespeare you say, the ever-lovin' Bard of Avon?"

"Uh, yeah. I guess," said Kat, vaguely remembering Jules using that nickname for him.

"You are in luck, my good lady!" said the clerk. "For just this very day arrived in the store a very special shipment indeed. I haven't even put it out on the shelf yet."

He reached under the counter and pulled out an enormous book.

"*The Globe Illustrated Shakespeare,*" said the salesman, reading the cover. "*The Complete Works, Annotated and Illustrated.*"

It was practically as large as Kat's family Bible that her grandma gave her on her first communion day a few years ago. But it was even more beautiful, if that were possible. It was bound in deep scarlet leather, with pages that had gold around the edges. Kat paged through the book and looked at all the notes and illustrations. Scenes from each of the plays were in vivid color that made even Kat want to read them.

As Kat was busy being dazzled by the book, she thought of Jules's pile of dog-eared paperbacks that filled her bedroom. Or that discount *Collected Works* Jules had bought used for $9.99 on eBay, and when it finally arrived, she had discovered there were markings all over the margins and some of the pages of *Hamlet* had been torn out. This would put them all to shame. This was the perfect gift on a birthday that really *needed* a perfect gift, especially after last night. Only how much could it be? This was not just a book; this was a work of art. Kat scanned the inside and outside cover looking for a price, but none was to be found.

She gulped, "Uh, how much is it?"

"Well, I haven't really priced it out yet," the bookseller replied. "It just arrived today, you see."

The old man could see Kat was doing calculations in her head and looking for an answer. "What might be your budget for this gift, young miss?"

"Uh, my mom said I could spend fifty dollars," Kat said,

knowing that such a treasure had to be more than that. "But," she said, silently adding up all the other cash she had in her purse, "I could go as high as...seventy-five dollars?"

The old man looked sternly from Kat to the volume of Shakespeare on the counter, doing his own set of calculations in his head. "Well, lassie," he said, "as luck would have it, this particular volume is exactly that, seventy-five dollars, tax included."

"You're kidding!"

"No," said the bookseller, sighing and seeming to be already calculating the loss he would be taking on the book, "I wouldn't kid about such a thing."

Kat plunked down the seventy-five dollars, and as it turned out, she had $77.95 in her purse. She insisted the clerk accept all of it, which he did. The bookseller wrapped the book in some special brown paper and the transaction was complete.

Kat thanked the man about twelve times and then left the store, clutching the special parcel tightly. She was elated because she knew in her heart of hearts that Jules was so totally going to love this and think it was the best present ever. It wouldn't hurt, of course, that as a side benefit of such an amazing gift, any lingering bad feelings Jules had toward Kat would certainly instantly disappear.

As he watched her go, the old clerk shook his head. "Mr. Sullivan will surely have my head for this one, glory be."

• • •

The next morning, Kat got up early to design the perfect combination of Glitter Girl stuff for her school debut. She had already chosen the nail polish, a color called Grape Jelly that went perfectly with the purple sleeveless blouse with the draped neckline that she'd been dying to wear to school since she'd seen it in the last edition of *Cosmo Girl*. A little subtle lip gloss, some slingbacks, and a pair of skinny jeans, and she was ready to roll.

Before she grabbed her backpack and headed out of the house, she grabbed the engineer's cap and put it on. She looked at herself in the mirror. She wasn't in love with that hat, but Chelsea had *strongly* suggested she wear it. Besides, she couldn't very well give it a great review on her blog and then *not* show up with it on her head on Monday. *It's just this once*, she thought.

She hopped into the waiting Prius in the driveway, said hello to Jules's dad, and then came face-to-face with Jules.

"Hi," Kat said, not really knowing what else to say. She was wishing today was Jules's birthday so she could give her the amazing present right now and all this awkwardness would be forgotten. Instead, Shakespeare was nowhere to be found, and Kat was left on her own in the back of the Prius. Jules looked over Kat's Glitter Gear as if she were looking at someone who had just refused to recycle a soda bottle.

"Uh, hi," said Jules, equally awkwardly.

"You didn't want to wear any of the stuff from the gift bag?" said Kat, who saw Jules had her usual jeans and T-shirt ensemble on today. This one was pale blue and had a stick figure on the front with a giant peace sign for a head. She'd worn this one before so Kat knew that on the back of the T-shirt in some outrageously large font size were the words "Think Peace."

"Oh, yeah," said Jules. "Some of that stuff wasn't really me. How was the rest of the party?"

"It was okay," said Kat simply, even though it had been one of the best sleepovers *ever.* "We tried out some other products and told Chelsea what we thought of them. I blogged a bit more. And then we all went to bed. Usual stuff."

"Yeah. I read your blog," said Jules simply. Kat felt a pang of embarrassment. Jules had read her review of the hat! Ick.

"You look nice, though," said Jules. Now she was the one not quite sure what to say.

"Thanks," said Kat. "You don't think it's too much purple?"

Jules thought Kat looked a bit like an eggplant being devoured by some kind of hideous pink bug, but all she said was, "No, you look nice."

They didn't talk much more than that for the rest of the ten-minute drive to school. Instead, Kat looked out the window and listened vaguely to Jules's dad's classic rock station that he always listened to when the girls were in the car.

They got to the school about ten minutes early, so most of the kids were still outside the building, milling around and talking. Jules and Kat got out of the Prius and slammed the doors shut. Looking out into the mass of students, they had one simultaneous reaction:

"O…M…G."

Wendell Willkie Junior High had been transformed into Glitter Girl Central. Every flavor of lip gloss was represented; every color of nail polish adorned someone's fingers or someone's toes. Girls were happily posing for pictures that they took with each other's Glitter Girl slam cams. And the hats! How many girls were wearing those Glitter Girl engineer's hats? Kat couldn't count them all. There had to be a hundred at least, and that was just in the eighth grade alone.

"Is this amazing or what?" said Kat.

"It's something," Jules had to admit.

"I guess Chelsea knows what she's doing."

"This isn't about Chelsea," said Jules. "This is about you, Kat. You must be very proud."

Kat was proud. Sort of. But in a way, it was a little creepy to see how many girls all looked the same. All of this because of what she had written on her blog less than forty-eight hours ago.

"Good day, ladies."

Kat and Jules turned around and froze. Standing before them was a completely transformed…Ms. Donovan? She had highlights in her hair and her trademark glasses had disappeared, replaced by contact lenses! For a change she was wearing a dress that didn't look like it could be pitched on a campground. And was that blue eye shadow?

"Ms. Donovan. Look at you. Wow! You've changed!" said Kat.

Ms. Donovan's cheeks flushed a little.

"Well, it occurred to me that I've had the same haircut since fifth grade, so I took your advice, Kat. I did the highlights, and while I was at it, I thought, what the heck… contacts!" Ms. Donovan's voice lowered. "I even bought some Glitter Girl. The eye shadow. I happened to be at the mall yesterday with my nieces. They begged me to go to the Glitter Girl shop—which, by the way, they loved—and talked me into it. Mouthwash, they call the shade. What do you think? Do I look okay?"

"You look—different," was all Jules could bring herself to say.

"But in a good way, right? You don't think the eye shadow's too much on an old gal like me?"

No, it didn't look bad to Jules. In fact, Ms. Donovan looked kind of pretty. But that wasn't the point. *This* was her Shakespeare teacher who practically spoke in iambic pentameter! And yet this maven of the Renaissance had caved in to Kat's pressure—the hair, the contacts, even the Glitter Girl! It would make your head spin if you weren't so busy throwing up.

"I think you look way cool, Ms. Donovan," said Kat, speaking up. "And the eye shadow rocks!"

"Well, thank you, Katherine. And I like your hat! I'm sorry I gave you a hard time about Glitter Girl. It seems like everything turned out okay, and the girls do seem to like it." Ms. Donovan turned to go, then quickly turned back.

"By the way, Jules!" Ms. Donovan said, pushing a strand of highlighted hair away from her face. "There won't be any Shakespeare Club today after school. Coach Scofield and I have a date, that is, a faculty meeting to attend."

Just as Jules was making a valiant attempt at digesting this information, the second bell rang. Time to get to class.

"I'll let you know about the new date for Shakespeare Club. It'll probably be next week sometime!"

As Ms. Donovan scurried down the hall she passed Coach Scofield, who was walking the other direction heading to the gym. And right on cue, Scofield swiveled his head around and watched the new-look Ms. Donovan move down the hall. Ms. Donovan must have sensed it, as Kat could see that she slowed down and was putting a little extra "cute" into her step as she walked away from him. This all during passing period, no less!

Jules looked at Kat, who was looking quite smug. And it irritated Jules more than a little bit. She shook her head as she turned and headed to class. Had the entire population of Willkie Junior High gone *insane*?

Chapter 12

The Course of True Love Runs
through the White Oak Mall

It was the absolute best day ever.

Everywhere Kat went, kids were stopping her, telling her how cool she looked or that they had read her blog (her traffic was up 500 percent!) and had gone out to buy Glitter Girl stuff. She had even gotten a text from Chelsea congratulating her—telling her every single item at the temporary Glitter Girl store they'd put up in the mall next to Ya-ya's Yogurt had sold out and that she, Kat, was responsible.

Kat didn't know if that meant she would be picked as the Face of Glitter Girl, but she knew it couldn't hurt. And it definitely went a long way toward subduing the extreme irritation she was feeling at having to wear that stupid hat all day long. It was hot, it was annoying, and who knew what it was doing to her hair? Why did she even bother using her root-lifting spray that morning? Habit, she supposed. Anyway, Kat didn't dare take the hat off, even for a second, for fear of what she might find up there.

Oh well, life was good in spite of the stupid hat, and she couldn't imagine how it could possibly get better.

Then she walked out the front doors of Willkie at the end of the school day and knew—oh yeah, life could definitely get better.

Kat usually hit the Sip N' Suds with Zoe and Darcy on Mondays. However, Jules's Shakespeare Club meeting had been canceled due to Ms. Donovan's suddenly coming down with a case of the "cools" so Kat was going to grab a ride home with Jules's dad instead. She really wanted to get home and cruise the Internet to see if she could get an idea of how the Glitter Girl launch campaigns in other cities had gone. She had thought about asking Chelsea but didn't want to seem overeager or desperate. Her mom always said, "Desperation is an emotion felt by losers. Winners feel expectation." Not that Kat *expected* to win, but she was sure hoping for it.

But her excitement to hop on her computer had been replaced by a whole other emotion she wasn't entirely familiar with—something like that feeling in the pit of your stomach just before you go over the first drop of a really high roller coaster.

Because when she walked out the front door of the school, instead of the Prius sitting at the curb waiting for her and Jules, she saw a classic red Mustang. Leaning against it was Kyle, his arms crossed over a white T-shirt that was so tight it showed the beginnings of his fifteen-year-old muscles. Because that's how old he was now, fifteen. In all the Glitter Girl fuss, Kat had forgotten it had been Kyle's birthday that weekend too. As Kat walked down the stairs toward him, he held up a set of car keys to prove it.

"Just got my learner's permit on Saturday. Want to go out for that burger?" asked Kyle.

And there it was. With those words, Kat's whole being began a free fall down the first hill of that impossibly tall roller coaster. Her face flushed, her heart leaped into her throat, and she felt a hot surge course through her body.

"Sure, but I have to be home by six. Adams totally slammed us with homework," she said casually so as not to betray her eagerness.

"Not a problem," said Kyle as he opened the front passenger door. Kat slipped in, smiling ear to ear.

"All righty, put your hands at nine and three o'clock and prepare to pull away from the curb, just like we practiced," came a voice from behind them. Kat's head swiveled around and she discovered that Mr. Finch was planted in the backseat. Ugh! Darn Indiana and its restricted licenses for teens! Kyle's dad *had to* be there, and unless there was an act of the legislature in the next five minutes, he wasn't going anywhere.

"Wait for me!" called Jules from the curb, hopping into the backseat next to her dad. Another passenger! Kat fumed in the front seat. Some date!

"So where are we headed?" asked Jules.

Ten minutes later, Jules stood deposited at the end of her driveway—feeling like so much discarded baggage—as the Mustang drove off.

She had waited all day for an apology from Kat. And if not that, at least a chance to ignore the incident and let things go back to normal, which had sort of been how they handled all their disagreements since the days of yore when they were still drinking out of sippy cups. But instead, Jules was left to stew in the backseat with her dad all the way home. Kat had barely spoken to her.

As Jules walked up the driveway to her house, she thought about just how complicated things would get if her brother and her best friend actually started dating. Yuck! The very thought of it made her skin crawl. And if she were really honest with herself, which she was not interested in being at the moment, she might admit that she was feeling more than just a little bit jealous of her friend and her popularity and her perfect day. And that was *not* good.

• • •

"This is sooooo good!" Kat exclaimed as she sipped on her nonfat Mangolade smoothie across from Kyle in a booth at Oh Donna's! '50s-style diner. Ten minutes earlier, Kyle's dad had finally disappeared into the home improvement section of the bookstore next door with instructions to text him when they were ready to leave, so it was almost like a real date now, which made the two teenagers relieved and a little nervous at the same time.

"Yeah, they're delicious," agreed Kyle. "And wait 'til you get a load of the french fries at this place. They're fantastic."

"I think it's so cool that your dad restored that car for you as a surprise. You must have been totally stoked when he gave you the keys this morning."

"Yeah. I have to say that as days go, this is one of the best ever," Kyle said in a dreamy sort of way that made Kat fairly certain he was including being here with her as part of that awesome day. Her stomach filled with butterflies as her whole being took another plunge on that internal roller coaster.

"So tell me about building those houses," Kat said, hoping to calm the butterflies with some conversation and another sip of her smoothie.

"It actually turned out to be pretty cool," Kyle said.

"I thought it was going to be totally lame—you know, a bunch of vegetarian goody-goodies running around with hammers and nails who didn't know what they were doing. There was some of that, but most of the volunteers were actually fun to hang out with. It made the work go a lot easier. And you know what the best part was? Seeing the families move into their new houses at the end. They were so grateful. Some of them even cried, they were so happy to have a place to call their own. It really made me feel good about what I had done all summer."

"Wow, that sounds really nice."

"Plus, I won a free Xbox in the employee raffle so, you know, that helped too."

Kat laughed at Kyle's joke but at the same time was impressed with the boy sitting across from her. He didn't seem at all like the annoying jock that Jules was always complaining about. "Yeah, we have to do some kind of volunteer work for school this year," she said, "but I soooo have no idea what I should do."

"Well, I think the program needs some local volunteers. You want me to give you the information?"

"That would be totally cool," Kat said, even though she didn't know a hammer from a stewed tomato.

"Maybe we could figure out a time to go together,"

Kyle said, smiling, "as long as you don't mind my dad in the backseat."

Kat smiled back at Kyle. Their eyes met for a moment, and then she looked away shyly.

Now that Kyle's dad was out of the picture, she had to admit that as first dates go, this had to be one of the best ever. She'd read about nightmare first dates in some of her teen magazines. All kinds of horrible things went wrong, like getting a huge zit on the end of your nose right before, or finding nothing to talk about and having awful awkward pauses, or saying something totally stupid or, OMG!, passing gas or burping in the middle of a kiss. But nothing like that happened on this date. No siree.

They ate burgers and played a few games at the Funtasia Family Arcade, where Kyle won her a plastic key chain with a heart on it, which she immediately hooked onto one of the belt loops on her jeans. They did a round of goofy golf, and Kyle had even put his arms around her to help her sink a putt on that really hard hole in the giant whale's mouth under the waterfall. And no one had a zit, and no one passed any bodily gases, and never once did they *not* have something to talk about. It was like they had known each other their whole lives, which, in truth, they had.

● ● ●

The sun was just beginning to set as Kyle pulled the Mustang toward the end of the cul-de-sac. It was 5:57 p.m. Right on time.

"Let me off here," said Mr. Finch from the backseat when they were still half a block from the house.

Kyle thought it might be some kind of test. "But I'm not supposed to—" he objected.

"I imagine you can navigate the rest of the way on your own, son," his father said, putting a firm hand on Kyle's shoulder. "Besides, I need to go check with O'Shea Building Supply to see if my drywall's in. Good night, Kat."

"Good night, Mr. Finch," said Kat, who was as unprepared as Kyle to be left alone so suddenly.

Kyle looked at her and shrugged and slowly maneuvered the car into the Connors's driveway, which Kat thought was so gallant. He could have just parked it in his own driveway which was, after all, just a few yards away, and made her walk. But no. He was a true gentleman and proved it further by getting out of the car and rushing over to open her door. He handed Kat her backpack, and they finally hit their first awkward pause. It wasn't like Kat was surprised. She had been thinking of this moment the whole entire date.

She wondered if he would want to kiss her—secretly

hoping with all her heart that he did. And if he did, how would she know it? Would he ask her first, like they showed you were supposed to do in those health training videos at school? Would he just move in with his head tilted at an angle? Or would there be that kind of magnetism she had seen a million times in romantic movies where the guy and the girl would just look into each other's eyes and find themselves locked in a sort of invisible tractor beam that would pull them slowly together until their lips met, their eyes closed, and the deed would be done? Then there was the issue of tongues—would there be tongues involved? And if there were, her stomach lurched as she suddenly worried that she might not be good at it!

Kat and Kyle looked at each other a moment. Kat finally broke the silence.

"Thanks. I had a really good time."

"Yeah. Me too. Would you, uh, like to go out again sometime?"

"I'd love to."

That was all the encouragement Kyle needed, because at that moment he went in for the kiss. It happened faster than Kat would have imagined. She almost didn't see it coming but that didn't matter because somehow, maybe on a cellular level, she was ready for it. And her lips met his with the sort of perfection in timing usually reserved for those triple axels in ice skating that ended in a flawless landing on exactly the right beat of music.

The kiss was soft and sweet and on the lips, without tongues. And it lingered for a moment, allowing them both to feel the warmth and excitement of it. Kat felt herself go all light in the head and was sure she was floating outside her body. When they finally pulled apart it was at exactly the same moment, so it didn't seem that one of them had chosen to end the kiss before the other.

Kat looked into Kyle's warm brown eyes that reminded her a lot of her favorite milk chocolate pudding. She felt a little embarrassed at what was at this point in her life the most intimate moment she had ever shared with another human being. Feeling her cheeks burn and her ears get hot, she quickly took her backpack and headed up the sidewalk. She heard the engine of the Mustang roar to life and paused to look back. Kyle waved as he drove the fifty feet from her driveway to his, parked the car, and went inside.

She turned back, took a deep steadying breath, and headed up to her house, which suddenly looked different to her. Her house that had seemed so huge most of her life suddenly seemed a little smaller. The steps that she once had to struggle up could easily be taken two at a time. The handrail that had felt so huge in her hand now fit so comfortably, as if it had been custom made just for her. Yes, something had changed, like maybe she was suddenly bigger. She didn't know when it happened. But she knew that at this moment, she noticed it. She wasn't a little girl anymore. And she really liked the feeling.

She bounded up the front steps, two at a time, and stopped in her tracks when she saw Jules sitting at the far end of the porch in the porch swing.

"Holy cow, Jules! You scared the life out of me! Have you been there the whole time?" asked Kat.

"Be nice to my brother, Kat. He's not just another accessory," said Jules.

Kat was appalled. Not only because Jules had been witness to her intimate moment, but because she would even make such a statement.

"Jules. How could you say that? You know me," said Kat defensively.

"I thought I did. I'm not so sure anymore," replied Jules and then got up and walked past Kat, down the steps, and into the darkening street.

Kat stood there stunned. She had no idea where this attitude was coming from. Okay, maybe she did. But she didn't want to think about it right now. The whole thing gave her a big, fat headache. She knew the cure and went into the house and headed straight to her computer.

Chapter 13

To Go or Not to Go,
That Is the Question

While Kat pounded out another blog entry singing the praises of Glitter Girl on her computer, Chelsea Ambrose was across town in her hotel room, looking into her laptop. She was in the middle of a video conference with the board of directors of Remoulet, Inc., back in Los Angeles.

"The tracking is off the charts," Chelsea said. "At every one of our temporary stores, we're hearing the same thing. From Maine to Miami, Glitter Girl is a hit. Traffic at the website is way up, and we're trending big-time on both Yahoo and Google."

Chelsea brought up some charts that she and her assistant, Amy, had put together that afternoon on the computer screen. Even though they were just pie charts and graphs, Chelsea thought the colors they had chosen added a certain feminine flair to the entire presentation.

"As you see here," Chelsea said, using her mouse to navigate among the charts, "sales of Glitter Girl merchandise in each of the fifty target markets have exceeded our projections. This buzz should build well for us as we get closer to our national launch next month."

Back in Los Angeles, Chelsea's charts were projected on a huge TV screen in the conference room on the thirty-fifth floor of the Remoulet office building. Gregory Remoulet nodded his head approvingly.

"Excellent!" he said. "It's clear that our trust in you was well placed, Miss Ambrose."

"Thank you, sir," said Chelsea, trying her best to be humble, which was about as easy for her as trying to be an iguana. Still, she thought she pulled it off. "I'm sure you're going to be equally pleased once we go national in November."

"Who says we have to wait until then?" Remoulet replied. "This is a brushfire you've started, Miss Ambrose. I say we keep it burning." He turned away from the screen for a moment. "Dave!" he barked. "How quickly could we get the Glitter Gear into the stores?"

"Well, I'd have to check with the suppliers, but I imagine if we shipped this week, we could have the stores stocked by the weekend."

"And what about the TV campaign?"

Chelsea couldn't believe what she was hearing. Were these executives actually talking about moving up the launch date of *her* little project? The project all her friends and colleagues had told her not to put too much faith in? What could make this any better? She had to pinch herself to make sure she wasn't dreaming.

"Wait a minute, sir! I have an idea!" Chelsea said, barely conscious that this was the time where she should just keep her mouth shut and let the more experienced executives work out the details.

All of the eyes in the boardroom in Los Angeles turned to the screen. Chelsea gulped. She had trusted her instincts so far, and she'd been right about everything. She might as well go all in on this idea.

"If we move up the date of the launch, we might as well take advantage of our Alpha Girls," she said. "Instead of just announcing the 'Face of Glitter Girl' on our website as we had planned, what if we brought all fifty girls to the same place, I don't know, an auditorium somewhere, we sold tickets, alerted the media…We could call it the 'World's Biggest Girl Party'!" Chelsea wasn't sure about that last part and couldn't really tell what the suits in LA were thinking about all this, but she was just rolling now.

"We're listening," Remoulet said in a way that Chelsea couldn't read.

"Everybody in the place would be in head-to-toe Glitter Girl," she went on, as the idea picked up momentum. "We could have bands and a DJ and music, and then at the end of the show…on live TV…we announce the winner of the Face of Glitter Girl contest!"

"Where would this show be?" Remoulet said, still not showing whether he liked the idea or not.

"How about Madison Square Garden in New York City?" said one of the suits in the room.

"Or Staples Center right here in LA?" said another.

"*No!*" said Chelsea, who surprised herself at how forcefully that word had come out of her mouth. "It has to be in the hometown of one of the girls. We're selling Glitter Girl as a line that *all* girls can enjoy and use. If we have it in New York or LA, it undercuts the products' accessibility to these girls, most of whom do *not* live in places with glamorous ZIP codes. We could have it at the gym at their school. Transform it into Glitter Girl Central for a day. It would be every girl's dream to be there. And it would be right in line with our overall viral strategy."

"Girl's got a point," was the general murmur around the room. Chelsea could have done without the "girl" part of the sentiment, but she was willing to leave that alone for the moment.

"But whose hometown? We've got fifty different girls to move," said one of the LA suits, who must have been an accountant. Leave it to those guys to throw cold water on a hot idea.

"This is Chelsea's baby," said Remoulet, calling her "Chelsea" for the first time that she could recall. "She should oversee the whole thing. You say your Alpha Girl was pretty good there in Indiana, did you?"

"Uh, yes, Mr. Remoulet. She's been great." For a brief moment Chelsea thought about the little flare-up with Jules at the party, but she quickly dismissed that thought.

"That settles it then. Miss Ambrose will run this show from her location. We need to get all the Alpha Girls there by the weekend. Dave, make sure she has all the resources of the company at her disposal."

"Sir, do you mean *next* weekend?" Chelsea said, already feeling the weight of the idea starting to settle on her shoulders.

"Is that a problem?"

"No, not at all, it's just…so soon."

"Make it happen, Miss Ambrose, and once you get back to Los Angeles, we'll have to have a long talk about your future here at Remoulet."

Chelsea knew what that meant: a raise and a promotion and an expense account with lots of zeros in it.

"Yes, sir, Mr. Remoulet," she said. "You can count on me."

"I know I can," Remoulet said. "And you can call me Greg."

ZZZT!!

Chelsea's screen went blank. The conference was over. She leaned back in her chair and stared at the ceiling. She had either been brilliant beyond words or just volunteered to oversee one of the biggest disasters in corporate marketing history, complete with her career suicide broadcast on live TV. It was too early to tell which. She took a deep breath and counted, "One…two…three." She picked up her cell phone from the table and dialed.

"Yeah, Amy," she said, kicking off her shoes, "I need you to book forty-nine flights to Indiana ASAP. And get out your pen. It's going to be a long night."

• • •

By the next morning, the event was starting to take shape. Chelsea had managed to book singer Jessica Aguirre, who had a concert in Chicago that weekend, to fly in and perform at the show. A few phone calls to Principal Neimeyer's office and a well-placed ten-thousand-dollar donation to the school library from Remoulet, Inc. was all it took to secure the school's gym for Saturday afternoon.

Glitter Girl's chief designer was flying in on Thursday to start decorating the gym. A press release had been sent to all the local media, as well as to Disney Channel, Nickelodeon, and FashionTV. Chelsea had even managed to call in a few favors from an old college friend in the TV business, and just like that, the whole event was going to be carried live on the new TeenZone cable network. The only thing left to do was to tell Kat Connors about it and let her blog do the rest.

Chelsea finally caught up to Kat after school at the Sip N' Suds, where she was hanging out with Zoe and Darcy.

"You're kidding!" Kat said when she heard the news. She could barely believe it. Did the fact the show was coming to Indiana mean *she* would be the Face of Glitter Girl? Chelsea didn't let on one way or the other. But it couldn't be a bad sign, could it?

Once Chelsea and her rented pink convertible had left the parking lot, Kat, Zoe, and Darcy squealed with delight.

"OMG! We are practically celebrities!" said Zoe, conveniently forgetting that *Kat* was the one in line to be the Glitter Girl. "This is going to be *amazing!*"

"I know!" chimed in Darcy. "It's positively magnanimous!"

The girls were causing such a ruckus that the laundry people on the other side of the Sip N' Suds turned away from their fluffing and folding for a moment to gawk at the trio.

The girls quieted down for a moment and flopped back down on the sofas. Kat dug in her purse and grabbed her phone. She had just added a cool calendar app that she loved and she wanted to put the Glitter Girl party on it right away, even though the chances of her forgetting the time and date of the party were approximately equal to the chances of her forgetting to breathe. She opened the app and quickly navigated her way to the date and time of the party: Saturday, October 15, at 2 p.m.

And there it was…in the special pink font she used for things she absolutely, positively couldn't forget:

JULES'S B-DAY
RENAISSANCE FAIRE
SATURDAY @ 2
DON'T BE LATE!

She checked the date and time twice, even though she knew it was right. In all the fuss and excitement of Chelsea's news, she had *totally* forgotten about Jules's party. Yet there it was, plain as day. At exactly the same time as the Glitter Girl party. She had been to every one of Jules's birthday parties since they were both in diapers. Kat sank deep into the cushions of the sofa, speechless. Now what?

Chapter 14

Cruel to Be Kind?

Kat didn't sleep all night. She tossed and turned. At one point she ran to the bathroom because she was sure she was going to be sick. Ultimately, it was a false alarm. Relieved, she laid her head against the cool porcelain tub next to the toilet. It took the edge off how crummy she was feeling and she actually started to doze off. But then suddenly the panic came back over her in a huge wave and her stomach tied up in knots again. She couldn't believe she was letting this stress her out so much.

Earlier that day, she had managed to get up the guts to call Chelsea and ask, even though she knew there was no way, if it was possible to switch the date of the big Glitter Girl launch party.

"You're kidding, right?" came Chelsea's irritated voice from the other end of the line.

"Well, I was just thinking that if you guys could change the date or the time just a little, it would work better for everyone."

"And who is this 'everyone' you're talking about?" Chelsea responded, pacing around her hotel room, getting more than a little annoyed. "It certainly doesn't work well for me or for the set designer or for Jessica Aguirre or for TeenZone or for any of the other girls who are flying here just for this event. Other than that, it works out just fine."

Kat sighed. She knew Chelsea would react this way, but she had to try.

"I guess you're right," she was forced to admit.

"Well then, what's so important that it's made you take your eye off the prize?" asked Chelsea.

Kat had hesitated in giving her answer because she knew how Chelsea would react. Chelsea didn't seem like the kind of person who had ever taken her eye off *any* prize, not in her whole entire life, not even for a best friend. Also, Kat was fairly certain Chelsea did not like Jules. Not after the scene she'd made at the party.

"Well?" Chelsea was waiting.

"I—uh—well it's the same day as Jules's birthday and I sort of promised I'd go." There. She'd said it. Then she closed her eyes waiting for the explosion. There was a moment of silence, then…

"Well, that does put you in a difficult position then, doesn't it?" Chelsea's voice was very calm. Not at all what

Kat expected. Maybe this was going to go a lot better than she thought.

"Yeah. And I don't know what to do exactly," explained Kat.

"I think it's obvious."

It was? Kat mulled it over a moment. Nothing. She waited for Chelsea to tell her, hoping the answer was an easy one.

"There's a choice that needs to be made," said Chelsea. And there it was. Obvious, but by no means easy.

"A choice," repeated Kat, disheartened.

"That's right. Life is all about choices."

"But it's so hard," said Kat.

"I know, sweetie. But it's the choices we make, particularly the tough ones, that define us."

Kat was silent. Chelsea was making sense, but it was the kind of sense your mom makes when she tells you to eat your broccoli.

"And if Jules was really as good of a friend as you say she is," continued Chelsea, "she would understand how important this is to you, how completely and utterly life-altering this could be, and *she'd* choose to change the date of her party."

What? Kat was suddenly thrown. She was so sure that

Chelsea was going to tell her that she had to choose not to go to Jules's party; it never occurred to her that it was *Jules* who had to make the choice.

"I never thought of it that way," said Kat.

"That's because you're a good friend, and you consider others first," replied Chelsea. "But don't you think you deserve the same consideration? After all, birthdays come every year. A chance like this is once in a lifetime. A real friend would see that."

Kat hung up the phone feeling a lot better and thinking that Chelsea was right. After all, if Jules *were* her BFF like she was always going around saying, she would understand and she'd do this one little thing for Kat.

• • •

"Are you crazy?! No, I can't change the date of my birthday! It's my birthday!" exclaimed Jules when Kat showed up at her house later that day. Jules paced up and down at the foot of her bed. "Why would you even ask me such a thing?"

"Well, you know this Glitter Girl thing I got picked for? They're doing this huge launch event for the whole line. And of every place in the whole country, they've decided they're going to have it here, Jules. At our school! They're flying in all the other Glitter Girl candidates—forty-nine other girls, one from each state. And they're going to announce the winner right here at Willkie! There's going to be media from all over. And they're going to air it live on TeenZone! Isn't that amazing?" said Kat, trying to make it sound as amazing and special as possible in the hopes that Jules would understand.

"And it's on my birthday," concluded Jules.

"Yeah."

"Unbelievable!"

"I know it's your birthday, Jules. But there's nothing that says you have to *have* the party on the actual day of your birthday."

"Nothing, except the fact I've already sent out invitations to everyone in Shakespeare Club *and* the Math Club. And my dad's already bought the tickets to the Renaissance Faire, which by the way are nonrefundable *and* it's the last day of the Faire. They're packing up and heading to Denver the next day!"

"Oh," said Kat. "Well, it sounds like you'll have a lot of people there to celebrate. You don't really need me too, do you?"

"Are you kidding me? Not have my best friend at my birthday party? We've never missed each other's birthdays!"

"I know, Jules. But this is really important to me. And if you're really my good friend, you'll understand how important," said Kat, throwing Chelsea's words at Jules. Only somehow they didn't sound as persuasive to Kat as when Chelsea had said them. Jules obviously didn't think so, either.

"Well, turning fourteen is a really big deal to me. And if *you're* really my good friend, you'll understand how important you being there is to *me*." Jules threw it right back in Kat's face.

And there it was. Two immovable forces at odds with one another.

Kat was perfectly ready to stand her ground, dig in her heels, and tell Jules that she was sorry, but she couldn't come and she would make it up to her somehow. Except, Jules burst into tears and Kat was totally unprepared for that. Kat had only seen Jules cry once, when her grandmother had died two Christmases ago. Now that had been a really big deal. Who wouldn't cry? Which made Kat realize how big of a deal this was to Jules, her being at the birthday party. Before she knew it, she had her arm around her friend, telling her there was no way she'd miss her party for anything in the world.

Now, hours later, lying on the bathroom floor in the middle of the night, Kat was miserable, not knowing what to do. On one hand, her conscience told her she had made a promise to Jules. On the other, the voices of Chelsea and her mom told her over and over that she had to do what was right for her.

She really needed somebody impartial to talk her through this. Her mom was too invested in this whole thing, and her friends would probably just tell her what they thought she wanted to hear. Then she got an inspiration. Her dad, the rational, no-nonsense businessman, would tell it to her straight.

She gathered herself off the bathroom floor, went to her room, and sat down at her computer. It was 4 a.m. in Indiana, but it was around lunchtime in Geneva, where Paul's latest venture had taken him. And even though he was in Switzerland, he *did* say that Kat could call him anytime.

Kat took a deep breath and used her computer to dial her dad's cell number.

"Kat!" Paul answered, sounding surprised by the interruption. "What time is it there?"

"Oh," said Kat, "it's kind of early."

"I can imagine. What's up?"

"Is this a bad time?" Kat said, not sure if she should have made the call in the first place.

"No, no. It's okay. I have a few minutes before I'm due at my meeting. What's going on?"

Kat launched into the whole story, leaving out no details. She spoke a mile a minute, picking up speed as she went. On the other end of the line, her dad said things like "Hmmm" or "I see" or "And then?" in a distracted kind of way that Kat couldn't quite read. So she just kept talking.

After she had told the story, which by the time she finished had more twists and turns than a Victorian novel, there was a long silence at the other end of the line. So long that Kat thought that she might have been cut off.

"Daddy?" she said. "Are you still there?"

"Yes, I'm here, Kat."

"Were you listening?" Kat said, starting to get a little frustrated.

"Of course I was."

"Well, what should I do?"

"It's not a matter of what you *should* do. You want to succeed in life, so you do what you *have* to do. Look at me. I make these kinds of choices every day. And look where it's gotten me. Look where it's gotten us. Our family," he said proudly.

Four thousand miles apart, thought Kat. She did not like that advice. Not one bit. Look where it's gotten their family indeed.

"Listen, Kat, Phil Mackenzie and Megan Burns just showed up. I have to run. Talk to you later. Love to Mom."

Click.

Kat slumped over the keyboard in frustration. That was no help at all.

Kat's stomach lurched again, and this time she really did throw up. Unfortunately, she didn't quite make it back to the toilet.

• • •

When Kat did not return Chelsea's phone calls or texts the next day, Chelsea knew something was up. She had been so sure that she had convinced Kat to ditch that schlumpy girl's birthday party. What fourteen-year-old girl in her right mind would even consider giving up an opportunity like this? She didn't like the fact that Kat seemed to have such a conscience.

It crossed her mind that Kat perhaps was not Glitter Girl material. But then the numbers kept coming in from the Indiana market and they were off the charts. So the girl had a conscience, so what? She also had charisma. She could deliver. She was an Alpha Girl. And Alpha Girls can't be made. They are born. Chelsea knew she had to do whatever had to be done to keep Kat in the pack.

• • •

Zoe slurped down the last of the White Chocolate Mocha Frappuccino that Chelsea had bought her and leaned back in her chair. They were tucked away in a tiny corner of a chain coffee shop that Zoe and her friends would normally never be caught dead in. It was strictly for soccer moms and middle-aged guys sporting Bluetooths and name badges on their way to work. Even so, when Chelsea had surprised her with a call asking Zoe to meet her after school to discuss a private matter, Zoe was so excited that the lameness of the location didn't bug her.

No, her thoughts were elsewhere. She thought for sure Chelsea had seen her own potential as a Glitter Girl and wanted to talk to her about it. It explained why Chelsea picked a place where none of the other girls would see them. Even though it crossed her mind that maybe she was going behind Kat's back in some way, Zoe didn't really care.

Sure, Kat was the obvious choice for Glitter Girl. She was really pretty and popular and always seemed to do, say, and wear the right things. But she'd be nowhere if it weren't for Zoe. Wasn't it Zoe who had told Kat about that new boutique off Sycamore that sold the awesome one-of-a-kind vintage dresses? And wasn't it Zoe who had given her the 4-1-1 on the messenger bag from Project Cool? It really irritated Zoe that after she told Kat and Kat had embraced those things, it was Kat who got all the credit around school for "discovering" them.

But Zoe kept her mouth shut because a lot of perks came with having Kat as a friend. As she sucked out the last few tiny, white chocolate chips that had stuck inside her straw, she was sure that Chelsea was going to announce that *she*, Zoe Palmer, was going to be the Face of Glitter Girl. And *that* would go a long way to launching her career as a pop star.

"You're probably wondering why I invited you here, Zoe," said Chelsea, sipping on her Venti Latte—skinny, of course.

Not really, but I'll act surprised when you tell me, thought Zoe, though she said, "Yeah. Sorta."

"Well, we have a problem."

Zoe shifted in her seat. This wasn't how she expected it to begin, the announcement that she was the Face of Glitter Girl.

"We do?"

"Yes. I think you know what it is."

Zoe had absolutely no clue what Chelsea was talking about. So instead of replying, she just chewed on the end of her straw.

"Jules," said Chelsea finally.

"Jules?" asked Zoe, staring straight at Chelsea, surprised.

"Yes. I'm afraid she's causing some serious problems with Kat and the whole Glitter Girl launch campaign."

Suddenly the images dancing in Zoe's mind of becoming the Face of Glitter Girl started to disintegrate.

"Jules is a loser," said Zoe, irritated now that she was sure this meeting wasn't turning out how she expected.

"You know that. And I know that. I'm afraid Kat doesn't seem to quite get it yet."

"Yeah. Kat's weird when it comes to Jules. They've been friends so long she doesn't see what everyone else sees. But I wouldn't worry about it. You just have to ignore Jules. It's what I usually do."

"Well, normally I would, but she's threatening to undermine the whole launch of Glitter Girl this Saturday," said Chelsea.

Zoe wasn't exactly sure what the word "undermine" meant, but she knew Jules. So she figured it had something to do with Jules causing a stink.

"You see, Jules's birthday party is the same day as the launch."

"So?"

"So. Kat promised she'd go to the party."

"And she's going?"

Suddenly Zoe was feeling hopeful again. If Kat was stupid enough to give up her Glitter Girl opportunity, that meant that Zoe could actually have the chance.

"Well, I'm not sure what she's thinking, frankly," said Chelsea, "but she absolutely has to be at the Glitter Girl launch. And since you're Kat's closest, best, and most important confidante and friend, I came to you because I knew you could help me make sure of that."

Zoe was irritated again. Why should she help Kat when she, Zoe, was the obvious choice for Glitter Girl?

"What difference does it make if Kat doesn't want to go?" Zoe said almost reflexively. "There are probably plenty of girls who'd be just as good, better even, at being the Face of Glitter Girl." *Including me*, she added in her mind.

"Perhaps. But the plans have been made. The press packets have been printed. If Kat doesn't go, well, let's just say I'll have to pull the plug on the whole thing and *no one* will be going." Chelsea made sure to emphasize the "no one" because she wasn't fooled for one second by this Zoe girl and her motivations. She would stab Kat in the back to get to the top. Chelsea actually liked that about her. Unfortunately, she had none of the innate style Kat had. She did have something Kat didn't have, though, and that was a desperate *need* to belong, to be part of the "in" crowd. Yes, Chelsea knew this girl well, because this girl was her customer. And Chelsea knew exactly how to prey on that desperation.

"Yes. If Kat doesn't go, we'll have to strike her from the program and take back all the backstage VIP passes she passed out. We might even have to change the venue to Chicago."

Zoe was horrified. Not go to the launch? Not be part of the VIP entourage backstage? No concert or giveaways or maybe even a chance to get her face in front of the cameras that were going to be there from every news channel? There was even a rumor that snarky celebrity blogger Gomez Endicott was coming to cover the event, and he was her absolute favorite! No, as much as she thought she was the perfect choice for Glitter Girl, she was not going to let this opportunity go down the drain.

"Well, I wouldn't want Kat to make a big mistake with her life. As her friend, I'll do anything to keep that from happening," said Zoe. "What do you need me to do?"

Chelsea held up a little flower pin. Zoe recognized it as one of the slam cams each of the girls had gotten in her goodie bag at the slumber party.

"There's something recorded on here that might eliminate our little problem," said Chelsea, and she smiled a smile that made a little chill go down Zoe's back.

Chapter 15

One May Smile and Smile, and Be a Villain

The countdown was on, and Jules was totally excited. A few days until her birthday and it was going to be the best one ever. Not only was Kat going to be there as planned, but it was taking place at her favorite event ever—the annual Renaissance Pleasure Faire—and most of the Shakespeare Club had promised to dress in period costume along with her. Ms. Donovan had even made arrangements for the club to head over to the high school before the Faire to check out its costume department.

Not only that, but the Willkie Madrigal Club, a Renaissance singing group that Jules was also a member of, had gotten picked to sing "Greensleeves." They were going to perform it just before the 3 p.m. jousting match to warm up the audience. Ms. Donovan told Jules to practice singing her solo part in the song extra loudly because the crowd at the Faire tended to be packed with bawdy revelers. Jules was totally stoked. She had sung solos before, but never in front of so many people. It was going to be great!

She was a little worried about Kat, though. They'd barely spoken since Kat had tried to bag on her birthday party a couple of days before. Jules felt a little bad about being so harsh to her. She knew how much the whole Glitter Girl thing meant to Kat. But shouldn't their friendship mean more? And what about giving your word? Kat had promised to come to her party long before the whole stupid contest came along. Besides Jules would never, ever bag out on Kat. So she felt she had done right by digging in her heels.

Still, as excited as Jules was every time she checked her computer and got a "will attend" RSVP on the Evites she'd sent out, eventually a little pang of guilt would trickle in. Not only about forcing Kat to miss the Glitter Girl launch, but it also occurred to Jules that Kat would really feel out of place at the Faire. It wasn't her scene, for sure. Then again, Jules suffered through a lot in the name of her friendship with Kat—Darcy and Zoe, to name two things. Still, would it be so horrible for Jules to let Kat off the hook? After all, Kat had proved her allegiance by choosing the birthday party over the launch. Anyway, they *could* have a second special celebration later.

Jules was having the whole debate in her head for the hundredth time that day as she sat down at her computer after school. Checking her Evite page was the first thing she did when she got up in the morning and when she got home from school.

She turned on her laptop and went straight for her emails to see if there were any new RSVPs when she noticed an anonymous email in her inbox. Because she didn't recognize the address she almost deleted it, but in the "subject" box someone had written "Jules. You are going to want to see this."

Puzzled, Jules clicked on the email. There was nothing in the body of the email—only a WMV video file attachment titled "With friends like these—"

She hesitated for a moment. She knew her dad had always told her not to open any attachment from someone she didn't know because of all the viruses flying around the Internet. However, this one seemed to be begging to be watched. Finally, Jules double-clicked on the attachment. Her media player automatically opened and a video appeared in the window. She was fully prepared to see one of those crazy videos that Sasha from Shakespeare Club occasionally sent her, like the Shakespeare's "Who's on First?" video, an Elizabethan twist on the old Abbott and Costello vaudeville routine. It was quite brilliant, she had to admit, and she was looking forward to something of equal amusement.

Jules sat back in her chair and sipped on her iced green tea as the video started. It took her a second to register that what she was seeing wasn't any spoof of the Bard. Instead, while it was something from out of the past, it was the very recent past, like last weekend. Specifically, the Glitter Girl slumber party last weekend. And the players weren't performers from the Internet, but Jules and Kat.

Jules stared openmouthed as she watched the argument that she and Kat had had unfold on the screen.

"Hey, stop. Don't be that way," Kat was saying as she chased Jules onto the front porch of the house. Whoever was videotaping had stopped at the foyer and, instead of following Kat out of the house, had moved to the front window. The window was open, so this secret video could therefore capture every word that was being said. Though it was dark outside, the porch light was on, and both Kat and Jules could distinctly be seen as well.

"What way? You mean be myself, unlike some people I know?" Jules watched herself spew the words and was a little surprised by how harsh she had sounded.

"I'm just having fun. What's wrong with that?" Kat had said as she pulled off her hat. Jules watched this feeling a little vindicated, knowing that Kat knew how stupid the hat looked.

"If being a sell-out is your idea of fun, I don't want any part of it," Jules had said and then stormed off.

A painful sense of embarrassment came flooding over Jules as she watched this, thinking maybe she had made too much of a scene. And maybe she even owed Kat a little bit of an apology of her own. Talk about being a drama queen. Yikes!

She fully expected the video to stop there, but it didn't. It kept going and whoever was shooting continued taping as Kat walked back into the house.

"I am soooo sorry for that whole scene," Kat seemed to say to the camera.

"I told you not to invite her," Jules heard Zoe's unmistakable snotty voice off camera. There were several murmurs of agreement. Jules was mortified knowing that apparently everyone had witnessed this scene.

"I guess I should have left her off the list like we had planned in the first place." Jules was stunned. She had suspected it that morning when Kat had gotten into the Prius and acted all weird toward her and avoided her all day. Her suspicions had been right on. And here was the proof, coming from Kat herself.

"Then why *did* you invite her?" It was Chelsea's voice this time. Jules wanted to know the answer as much as

Chelsea obviously did. So despite the hurt she was feeling, she kept watching.

"Well, I don't know, I—uh—her brother was standing there—"

"Her brother *is* really cute," Zoe again, offscreen.

"Yeah. And I felt guilty. And, and I guess, I guess it was like a, you know, a pity invite!" said Kat.

ZZZT! And the video clip ended. Jules sat there, her face hot and red, a burning feeling in her chest, tears swimming in her eyes. A pity invite? That's what she was? That's the only reason Kat had invited her? That, and trying to impress her dumb brother?

The words stung. They produced actual physical pain, as hurtful as if she had been slapped in the face. And coming from her best friend too. Someone who was supposed to be her best friend anyway. It made the pain all the more unbearable.

After the shock began to wear off, Jules slumped over. She buried her face in her hands and began to cry; deep, chest-rattling sobs that came from her very core.

"Hey. You okay in there? I thought I heard crying," came Kyle's voice from the other side of her bedroom door.

Jules mustered her best normal voice. "Nah. It was just a video I was watching." Jules listened for a moment and then she heard Kyle's footsteps recede down the hall.

When she was sure he was out of earshot, Jules made her way over to her bed. She flung herself onto it, burying her face in her pillow, and cried for a very, very long time.

Chapter 16

The Winter of Kat's Discontent

The next morning, Kat woke up early. Not that she'd done a whole lot of sleeping the night before. She'd seen a segment on the *Tracy Mulholland Show* after school a few weeks before where some doctor told Tracy that most teenagers were sleep-deprived. After the last few days, she could believe it.

But this morning, she finally felt like she knew what she had to do. If there had been any doubt in her mind, the conversation with her dad had convinced her. She'd call Chelsea as soon as school was out and let her know she had decided to attend Jules's birthday party. It would hurt like heck to say so and to miss out on the cool launch party, but they *did* have forty-nine other Glitter Girl candidates to choose from. Chelsea could surely round up another girl from Indiana if they needed one. Maybe even Zoe. It wasn't like she was a lock to get the thing anyway.

She headed down the stairs and grabbed a low-fat yogurt from the fridge. She was on her own on Wednesday mornings. Her mom had an early Pilates class, and her dad wouldn't be back from Geneva for at least another week. As Kat dug into her morning yogurt, she unplugged her cell phone from its charger next to the TV. She loved her smartphone, but it did suck up the battery life so quickly that if she didn't charge it every night, she'd be without a phone the next day. For Kat, that was the same as being without some other little accessory in her life like, say, oxygen.

Beep! Beep!

The cell phone sprang to life, announcing a text message that had come in at some point after she turned off the phone the night before. There was just one message there. It was from Jules.

> Got 2 go in early today. Shakespeare stff. Can't give u ride.
> Sorry. TTYL

Huh? Jules almost never bagged out on giving her a ride. And why hadn't she just called last night? What's *that* about? Her mind immediately filled with thoughts of Jules trying to pull some kind of fast one on her, or Jules avoiding her altogether. But by the time her mom got back from Pilates, Kat had almost convinced herself that it had nothing to do with the weirdness between them the last few days.

"Kat? Are you sick?" her mom asked, dropping her

car keys into a dish next to the door. "First period has already started."

"Yeah, I know, but Jules couldn't give me a ride today, so I was kind of stuck here until you came back."

"Honestly, today of all days." Her mom sighed, grabbing the keys again and turning back toward the garage.

The ride to school was uneventful, except for her mom's speech about how Jules shouldn't be so selfish and how it was important for everyone to do their fair share. Kat thought it would have been a more powerful point if her mom had given them a ride to school more than a handful of times since the beginning of the year. But her mom was rolling, and she was never one to let the facts get in the way of her complaining and indignation.

First period was almost over when Kat arrived at Willkie, which meant that she had to go to Assistant Principal Noble's office to get a tardy slip, something that she hated to do. Luckily Mr. Noble wasn't there, so she was spared one of his lectures about punctuality, and she only had to deal with the attendance secretary, Mrs. Vettorazzi, who was always super nice, no matter how late you were.

By the time Kat secured the tardy slip, the first period bell had already rung, and passing period was nearly over. That meant she wouldn't see Jules until lunch. Even though Kat knew she'd chosen to do the right thing by going to Jules's party, somehow it didn't feel right. She couldn't help thinking that Jules was ruining what should have been the best time of her life. She didn't *like* thinking that, but there it was, just the same.

The two periods until lunchtime dragged on. It took seemingly forever for Ms. Jolly to explain how to count a dotted eighth note in music class. Then in computer class, Kat had to sit through five boring PowerPoint presentations her classmates had designed the week before. Boring PowerPoint presentations were bad enough, but today's were particularly painful. Travis Gilroy had decided to use every transition in the entire software program, so it took *forever* to get from one slide to the next, and Angie Ferris still didn't know how to get her presentation to play without a lot of help from Ms. Cardiff. But eventually and mercifully the bell rang and it was time for lunch.

By the time Kat had worked her way through the lunch line and grabbed a Caesar salad and some applesauce, Zoe and Darcy were already sitting at their usual table. Jules was nowhere to be seen, but that wasn't so surprising. Jules was a vegan and didn't eat any meat or dairy products, so she always brought her own lunch to school and never went through the line with the other students. Sometimes she had eaten her entire lunch with the other brown baggers before Kat ever made it through the line, but she would usually turn up at their table when she finished. Kat scanned the lunchroom, and she saw the usual tables. There were the volleyball girls hanging out with the football boys. Then there were the band members sitting with the kids from show choir. And then…Jules. Sitting by herself. Not even with the Shakespeare Club.

"Come on, you guys," Kat said to Zoe and Darcy. "Let's go sit with Jules."

Darcy dutifully jumped up, but Zoe sat glued to her seat as if she were held down by a giant magnet.

"Come on, Zoe," Kat said. "Lunch is almost over."

Zoe slowly got up and followed two steps behind Kat and Darcy. She would have preferred not to be around when the explosion occurred, like computer hackers who never saw the destruction they caused. But as long as it was going to go down right here at lunch, she might as well get a good look at it.

Kat plopped down next to Jules at the table.

"What did you guys do in Mr. Adams's class today? I totally didn't get that worksheet he gave us for homework," she said, completely unaware of the storm that had been growing inside Jules since the night before.

"OMG. Me neither," said Darcy. "It was like completely amorous."

Jules said nothing. She couldn't believe it had come to this. Here she sat in the middle of her junior high lunchroom with her so-called best friend prattling on about science class as if nothing were wrong. And those two phonies, Zoe and Darcy, hanging on her every word. And Darcy abusing the English language beyond all recognition. As she stared at her half-eaten apple tofu spring roll, a quote from Shakespeare came into her head:

"If it were done when 'tis done, then
'twere well it were done quickly."

Jules had memorized the passage from *Macbeth* two semesters ago, but it somehow stuck in her head all these months later. In the play, the character Macbeth was talking about murdering the King of Scotland, but it was a good quote for almost anything, Jules thought. Do it now. Get it over with.

"Maybe Mr. Adams will have pity on you," she said. "Seems there's a lot of that going around these days."

"What do you mean?" said Kat. "Hey, Zoe. You going to eat all your fries?"

"I can't believe you," said Jules. "Are you seriously just going to sit here and mooch Zoe's french fries as if nothing happened?"

"What's supposed to have happened?"

"I got an email with that video."

"What video?"

"Has that Glitter Girl stuff seeped into your cerebral cortex and affected your brain?" said Jules. She reached into her book bag and produced her cell phone where she had stored the video she'd been sent. She practically shoved the phone into Kat's face and pressed "Play."

Kat watched the video in disbelief.

"Who sent you that?"

"What does it matter?" said Jules. "Probably somebody who wanted me to know what my so-called BFF says when I am out of the room."

"That video is soooo out of context."

"What context? Are you going to deny you said it?"

"No, but I didn't really mean it like that."

"Like what? I was a *pity* invite? What am I, a stray puppy to you?"

Kat had never seen Jules this upset. The only thing she could do was to try for damage control.

"All I was trying to say was that Glitter Girl wasn't your

thing, and it probably was a bad idea to invite you in the first place."

"And maybe it was a bad idea for me to be your friend for the last twelve years. I don't want to be around someone who sees me as some pathetic loser."

"I don't see you like that, exactly."

"*Exactly?* Well, what exactly do you see me as?"

"What are you talking about? You're my friend. My best friend," Kat added quickly, even though she knew Darcy and Zoe were watching this whole thing from three feet away.

Jules couldn't stand to be around Kat any longer. She grabbed her lunch and left the table. Kat chased after her. This was *not* going well.

"Wait!"

"For what?" Jules said. "Why don't you just hang out with your *real* friends and leave pitiful me alone? Maybe you guys can get together with Misty Wilkins, and you can trade mascara or discuss blue eye shadow or try on some more pathetic hats."

"Look. I'm sorry I said those things on the video. I don't know who sent that to you, but I didn't mean for it to come out like that. Come on, Jules, you know me."

Jules stopped short. That's just what Kat said after she'd

traded spit with her brother. "*Know* you? I thought I did. But the Kat I know doesn't sell herself to the highest bidder just to get a little fame. The Kat I know was cool and had her own style, and doesn't let anyone tell her what to do or who to hang out with. Look at you. Ever since Chelsea came to town, you've let yourself get turned into a little Glitter Girl clown. Not even a clown. You're a mannequin. Brainless and heartless and made of plastic. A mannequin."

"You take that back!"

"I won't. Mannequin!"

"Shut up!"

"*Mannequin!*"

Jules was shouting at the top of her lungs now. A crowd of kids had started to gather around the two girls. The possibility of a classic catfight filled the lunchroom air, and nobody wanted to miss a thing.

Kat noticed that they were being watched and knew she had to dial back the tension a bit.

"Look, you can scream mean things if you want to. I'm not going to apologize for being popular with the other girls."

"What do these girls even know about you beyond that ridiculous hat? Do they know you love peanut butter and celery? Do they know you sometimes get scared when you're in that big house all by yourself? Do they know how it upsets you when your parents argue? Or how you cry sometimes cuz your dad's not around? Do they know any of that stuff? We're more than friends. We're blood sisters. Remember?"

"That was when we were five years old, and it wasn't blood. It was cherry Kool-Aid!"

"An oath is an oath!"

"Well, maybe I've outgrown those oaths," Kat said. "Maybe I've outgrown a lot of things."

"Fine! And maybe I've outgrown *you*! Don't even think about coming to my birthday party! There! I've saved you the trouble. You can go to your little Glitter Girl party on Saturday with a clear conscience. You're officially uninvited!"

Jules turned on her heels and stormed out of the lunchroom, angrily tossing her unfinished lunch into the trash. With the chances of a catfight off the table, the crowd of kids started to disperse, leaving Kat standing by herself in the middle of the room.

Not quite knowing what to do, she looked around and saw Zoe and Darcy standing by the benches. They had witnessed the whole thing. Zoe walked over to Kat and gave her a big hug. Only Kat didn't really feel like hugging anybody at the moment.

"Come on," said Zoe. "Let's get some fresh air."

The three girls started to walk out to the schoolyard.

"I didn't know you liked celery and peanut butter," Darcy said.

"Shut up, Darcy," said Zoe.

"Well, did *you*?" Darcy said to Zoe as they approached the door.

Kat pushed open the heavy metal door that led to the schoolyard. The bright noon sunshine hurt her eyes. She could barely see.

Kat was numb. Just numb.

Chapter 17

What's Done Cannot Be Undone

"Okay. Who sent it?" Kat looked angrily from Darcy to Zoe.

"Who sent what?" asked Darcy. Kat blinked in disbelief. Was Darcy really that clueless, or was this just a clever ploy to deflect suspicion?

"The video, Darcy," she snapped, "the one Jules was so upset about thirty seconds ago? Are you even on this planet *ever*?"

"Hey. Don't come down on Darcy cuz Little Miss Birkenstocks got her tie-dyed undies all in a bunch!" Zoe jumped to Darcy's defense, not out of guilt but because it peeved her royally that Kat just *assumed* it was one of them. Which of course it was, but still.

"There were like twenty girls there who could have taken that video," continued Zoe, mustering as much indignation as she could to make sure to throw Kat off her scent. "Remember, we all had slam cams! But you're blaming us? That is so over-the-top wicked. You want someone to blame, maybe you should blame yourself!"

"Me? Why? I didn't send it to her!" Kat said, slinging the indignation right back at Zoe.

"No. But you *said* those things," replied Zoe.

The indignation began seeping out of Kat like the air in a balloon punctured by Zoe's point.

"But I–I didn't, you know, mean them. Not really."

"Oh puh-lease. You told us yourself you didn't think Jules belonged at the party. You weren't even going to invite her! You only changed your mind cuz you were afraid Kyle wouldn't be so hot on you if you left his little sister off the list."

"That's so not true! I–I invited her because she–she's my friend." Even as Kat said the words, she knew they didn't taste true coming out of her mouth.

"You know what? I don't know who sent that video. But whoever it was did you *and* Jules a big favor. Now you can finally ditch her dead weight. And she can finally know that you're really not her friend. Come on, Darce. We've got more important things to do than hang out where we're not trusted." Zoe turned and walked off.

"We do? Like what?" asked Darcy as she chased after Zoe.

Whatever numbness Kat had felt as a result of her fight with Jules was quickly wearing off. And now she was feeling everything all at once—hurt and guilt and shame that all added up to a general sense of ickiness. So she did the only thing she could think of doing. She ran. Hard.

She didn't know where she was going at first. She just felt like she had to do something to make herself feel better. When she finally stopped and bent over to catch her breath and to work out the stitch in her side, she realized that she had run to the gym.

The gym had been declared strictly off limits as soon as the Glitter Girl crew showed up to set up for the show, but a lunchtime pickup game was in full swing at the outdoor basketball courts nearby. Kat found herself looking around desperately for Kyle in the sea of tall, lanky boys. Yes, this is where she was headed all along, even though she hadn't consciously realized it at first.

She spotted Kyle standing off to the side, wiping the sweat off his face with his T-shirt and downing a Gatorade. Already Kat was breathing a little easier and it wasn't from just catching her breath. She'd talk to Kyle and explain everything, and he'd totally get it. He'd know what to do because he'd known both Kat and Jules, well, forever. He would know how to smooth things over with Jules, and everything would go back to the way it was.

Kat caught Kyle's eye and she waved and smiled at him. But he didn't wave and he didn't smile back. He just gave her a cold stare and rejoined the game, running down the court on a fast break. He could have looked over at her at any moment, even for a second. But as Kat stood there watching him play, she *knew* that he was not looking at her on purpose.

Kat felt like she had been slapped in the face. It was a diss. A definite diss. There was no other way to explain it because there was no way Kyle hadn't seen her. He had looked her right in the eye and then just got up and started playing! Suddenly it occurred to Kat that Jules must have shown the video to Kyle.

Kat felt foolish for thinking that Kyle would show allegiance to her above his own sister. And if Kat were honest with herself, she couldn't blame him. That video made her look pretty bad. And if she were *really* honest with herself, she'd have to admit that she was to blame for just how bad she looked. The words had, after all, come out of her mouth. She didn't *have* to say them. She *chose* to. Sure she had felt pressured to say them. But that was no excuse. Was it?

Kat felt the tears welling up in her eyes. Even though Kyle was doing everything he could *not* to look at her, Kat couldn't let Kyle see her like this. She ducked behind a bank of bleachers that had been removed from the gym to make room for the Glitter Girl stage, and started to cry. She'd lost her best friend, ticked off her other two BFFs, and lost her boyfriend all in the course of thirty minutes. On the suckiness scale, this afternoon clocked in at totally abysmal. Kat put a hand to her mouth to stifle the sobs that were coming quick and hard now.

Suddenly, she heard footsteps and voices coming from the other side of the bleachers near where she stood. She held her breath and leaned back against the wall of the school, not wanting to be heard. But she could hear the voices on the other side of the bleachers very distinctly.

She recognized one voice as belonging to Coach Scofield. The other was that of Assistant Coach Deevers, her balding geometry teacher, whose tangled front teeth forever looked like he'd just eaten a bagel and had forgotten to brush.

"You and Donovan? You gotta be kidding me. I bet she hasn't had a date since her brother took her to the senior prom," said Coach Deevers, laughing the same mean laugh that some eighth-grade boys did whenever Carrie Mitchell, the girl who weighed two hundred pounds, walked by them. That always made Kat sooo mad. Why hadn't she ever said anything? Jules always did.

"Yeah, I know, right? I don't understand half the stuff that comes out of her mouth. She talks like those old bags that give you tours in a museum or something. Not that I've ever been," Scofield added quickly. "I only heard."

"So why bother?"

"Cuz I'm new in town and she's way eager to show me around. And she's one of them feminist types where she even pays a lot of the time."

"No way!" Deevers laughed that mean laugh again.

"Yep. At least until basketball season is over and I have time to meet some real chicks, I figure why not? I mean, she's available, she's not wearing those dorky glasses anymore, and she did something better to her hair. I'm not sure what."

"Still, Donovan, that's scraping the bottom of the barrel."

"Yeah. But free drinks," and then they high-fived and they *both* laughed that awful, mean laugh. Kat felt the blood rise in her face, just like she did whenever she saw Carrie get tormented. And she wanted to say something to these jerks, she really and truly did. But she didn't. Not like Jules would have done. In the end she just ran into the school building as fast as she could.

Kat walked down the empty hallways, her footsteps echoing, making her feel even more alone than she already felt. She couldn't believe what she had heard in the gym. Coach Scofield didn't even *like* Ms. Donovan. He was *using* her, and Kat was 100 percent responsible for throwing them together. What had she done? She thought about what Jules would say about this, and it involved a million "I told you so's" and probably a serious lecture or two.

That's if Jules were talking to her, which she wasn't. Somehow Kat was relieved about that because she couldn't take it, not right now. Not after all that had happened. But then again, she really wished she had someone to talk to and normally that someone would have been Jules. Kat felt really lost, with nowhere to turn.

Then, as if the universe had heard her anguish (and let's face it, how could it not, as badly as Kat was feeling at the moment), Kat saw it. The hot pink Mercedes with chrome wheels was parked right in front of the school as Kat exited. And standing there, leaning against the hood checking her BlackBerry, was Chelsea. She looked up and saw Kat and gave her the biggest, warmest, most welcoming smile, and Kat completely broke down in tears again. Chelsea rushed over to Kat. "Oh sweetie, what's wrong?"

Kat just sobbed.

Chelsea put a comforting arm around her. "What do you say you and me play a little hooky?"

The next thing Kat knew, the two of them were sitting at a little bistro table outside the Café Olé in the White

Oak Mall having mochaccinos. Kat bared her soul about everything that had happened. It came out in a torrent as she told Chelsea about the video and her blowup with Jules, about her accusations of Zoe and Darcy, and what she overheard Coach Scofield saying about Ms. Donovan. At one point Kat got so upset that she accidentally knocked over her drink. By the time it was all done, more than a few tears (and a considerable amount of chocolate-flavored espresso) had been spilled.

"Look, honey," Chelsea said finally. "I know it hurts, this whole thing with your friend, but the truth is, relationships change. It happens to everyone. I mean, I don't even talk to my mother anymore."

"You don't talk to your mother?" Kat asked dumbfounded.

"It's a long story. Anyway, it's clear to me and practically everyone else who knows you that you've outgrown Jules."

"But we were such good friends."

"When you were kids. But you're not a kid anymore. You're a young woman who is becoming her own person with her own sense of style and direction in the world. And your friend, if you can call her that, doesn't approve of your choices and she's making you feel horrible about them, isn't she?"

"Yeah, I guess so."

"Well, a good friend would accept you for you who are and not judge you and certainly not jump down your throat for telling the truth."

Chelsea made a good point. Still—

"But who sent her the video?"

"What difference does it make? The point is, they did you *and* her a favor because this has been a long time coming."

"That's exactly what Zoe said," said Kat.

"And she's right! Let me tell you, sweetie, you weren't doing Jules any favors by allowing this friendship to linger, because, let's be frank, she will never be in your league. She would only hold you back and end up getting really hurt herself somewhere down the line," said Chelsea.

Kat mulled this over as she took the last sip of her drink, trying to process what Chelsea had just said. But before she had the chance—

"Hey, you know what always makes me feel better when I'm blue?" Chelsea asked. Before Kat could answer, Chelsea flipped out the shiniest, sleekest-looking silver credit card. "A shopping spree…on the company card."

Chelsea smiled and grabbed Kat's hand. "We'll start with a makeover. Then I saw this gorgeous little ruffled dress in the window at Forever 21."

As Chelsea's heels clacked past the straight iron kiosk toward Sephora, Kat had no choice but to scramble after her.

Chapter 18

The Readiness Is All (Plus a
Really Kickin' Sound System)

The next few days passed for Kat like they were some kind of bizarre dream. Everything was upside down. She was getting her rides to school from her own mom now, and she could barely remember the lie she had told to explain why Jules had suddenly stopped being around. Something about Kyle practicing with the Mustang on the way to school and his license and their parents not wanting Kyle to have any distractions when he still only had his restricted permit, although Kat would be hard pressed to re-create that lie even if you gave her a whole day to think about it.

Meanwhile, Kat couldn't stop obsessing about who had sent the video. She had already concluded that neither Darcy nor Zoe could have taken it. She remembered that you could see Darcy in the corner of the shot at the end, and you could hear Zoe's voice, which sounded far away, not that weird close sound that the person who's taking the video always has. And if neither of them *took* the video, it was hard to believe one of them had sent it. That would be a "Let's screw up Kat's life" conspiracy to rival all others. With her two BFFs back in the fold, it took a little of the sting off the dustup with Jules. Instead Kat was trying to look forward to the launch party as much as she could.

"I heard another ad for the launch party on the radio," Darcy said at lunch just two days before the event. "Those ads are, like, on more than the songs now."

"Did you guys hear Jessica Aguirre's new single?" Zoe asked. "I just downloaded it. It's totally sick. I wonder if she's going to sing that one on Saturday."

"Jessica Aguirre has a weird nose," said Darcy, giving her best shot at music criticism.

"Yeah, but at least she doesn't have acne!" Zoe said, mocking the scene from the infomercial that all the girls had seen about a billion times. "Does your skin cause you embarrassment? Do people scream when they see you coming? Do your pets cower in fear when you open the door to your house? That happened to me too, before CleanSweep from Remoulet!"

Zoe and Darcy cackled and howled. Kat just watched them. Usually a good joke mocking a teenage celebrity would be right up her alley, but today, she wasn't up for it. She had thought it would be totally uncomfortable to go to school and have to interact with Jules all day long. But it wasn't awkward at all. Instead Kat finally realized how little they actually hung out anymore…unless they made a point of it.

They were only in three classes together, and even then, they sat on opposite ends of the room. Then, at lunch, Kat usually let Jules eat her vegan stuff with her brown-bag crowd, and their paths hardly crossed in the hallways. It was a big school, after all. After school, it was the same thing.

Jules and Kat hadn't done the same after-school activities since fourth grade, when their parents pushed them both to sign up for the junior volleyball team. Even then, the only thing they had agreed upon was what a *horrible* idea it had been in the first place. So here was Kat fully expecting to be missing her friend, only to realize she wasn't around that much to miss. Weird. Maybe Chelsea was right, after all.

When the girls walked by the gym on the way back to class, they noticed two enormous trucks bearing the logo of some production company from Chicago parked outside. Guys who looked like they knew what they were doing wheeled equipment off the trucks and into the gym. To the starstruck Zoe, it looked like catnip.

"Come on," she said. "Let's check it out."

"Guys, passing period's almost over!" Darcy protested. "I don't want to get busted."

"Oh come on, what's the worst that could happen?"

"One of those big spotlights could fall on my head and leave me permanently brain damaged?"

"How would we tell the difference?" said Zoe under her breath.

Zoe wasn't in the mood for a debate at the moment. So she did what every girl in her position would do—appeal to authority.

"Kat, don't *you* want to see what's going on?"

Kat smiled. A little adventure could be just the thing right now.

"Let's do it."

"Ka-a-a-a-a-a-t!" Darcy said, adding about twenty-eight syllables to her name.

"Relax, Darcy," Kat said peeking around the corner. "You know Ms. Tate is barely awake after lunch. She won't even notice if we walk in a few minutes late."

That was good enough for Darcy.

"Okay," said Kat, changing into full Alpha Girl mode for a moment. "You guys follow me. Kyle showed me a secret passage into the gym through the visitors' locker room."

"And just what were you doing exploring secret passages with Kyle?" Zoe asked.

"Shhh! I think I heard something!" Kat hadn't heard something, of course, but discussing Jules's brother at this particular moment rated high on the bummer-ocity meter.

Kat led the girls down a narrow passage behind the same stack of temporary bleachers where she had witnessed Coach Scofield and Coach Deevers having their conversation a couple of days earlier. At the end of the passage was one of those fire doors that you absolutely, positively weren't supposed to open unless the school was under a nuclear attack.

"You're going to sound the alarm if you push that!" a still spooked Darcy said.

"Then shield your ears, Darcy, cuz here we *goooooo*!"

Zoe and Darcy dived behind Kat and cowered, expecting one of those ship horns like they had on the *Titanic*. Or at the very least one of those horrible noises that some fire trucks make in old foreign movies.

Instead, nothing.

Kat smiled and gently pushed the door to the visitors' locker room open.

"You knew that was going to happen!" said Darcy.

Kat laughed. "Of course I did. The janitor disarms it so

he can get from one end of the school to the other without having to tramp through the halls. Come on."

The faint stench of unwashed socks filled the air as the trio tiptoed through the locker room. They peeked out of the door to the gym, doing their Nancy Drew best to avoid detection. Since the production company had showed up the day before, nobody had been allowed to enter and all gym classes had been stuck playing softball out in Foley Field on the other side of campus.

As the girls took cover behind a rack of folding chairs, Kat could see why.

The gym had been transformed. Totally transformed. And not crummy transformed like when you have to decorate for the fall dance, and you've only got a three-hundred-dollar budget for the whole thing and nobody wants to volunteer, so the best you can come up with is a lot of crepe paper decorations and glitter on signs. This was like Hollywood!

A huge stage had been constructed in the place where the pep band usually sat during the basketball games. It must have been thirty feet wide. Behind the stage, workmen were putting up a giant video screen so everyone could see no matter where they were sitting. Gigantic banners advertising Glitter Girl products were being hoisted into position on huge ropes. It was a massive operation—a shrine to teen beauty and style. Kat, who had just studied ancient Egypt in social studies class, whispered to herself.

"It's like they're building the pyramids at Giza."

"Only this isn't for King Tut," Zoe answered in a whisper. "This is all for you, Kat."

Kat had been so caught up in the drama of the last few days that she had almost forgotten about the Face of Glitter Girl contest. But it was true. She could be the Glitter Girl, just as easily as any of the other forty-nine girls. And the way Chelsea was talking when they went to the mall, maybe even easier. She could barely allow herself to believe it. Her face on magazines, on TV even.

"Guys, look!" Zoe whispered excitedly, pointing toward the stage.

"Wow, a giant shampoo bottle!" said the easily impressed Darcy.

"No, behind that, it's Jessica Aguirre!"

Sure enough, there she was. Among a sea of what Kat took to be stage managers and producers was the teen queen of pop herself. You'd barely recognize her without the belly shirt, short shorts, and metallic boots. She was dressed in a denim jacket, jeans, and a plain white T-shirt as she shook hands and listened quietly to the producers explain something about the upcoming show. She looked like, well, a teenager.

"Gosh, she's so beautiful," said Darcy, apparently forgetting her comments from just twenty minutes earlier.

"This show is going to be great!" squealed Zoe under her breath.

Looking around at the massive construction project underway at her school, Kat could hardly disagree. There wasn't much that could make this better.

Well, maybe one thing.

• • •

Just as Kat predicted, the girls managed to sneak into Ms. Tate's class undetected before she had even bothered to take the roll. The lesson that day was on avoiding something called dangling participles, which couldn't be good with a name like that. As far as Kat was concerned the only things that should be dangling were earrings. However, fresh from their adventure in the gym, Kat couldn't concentrate on participles of any kind. Seeing the preparations made her more sure than ever that she was right to trust Chelsea and ignore her gut and go to the launch party. Still, whenever she thought about Jules, who at this moment was sitting at the back of the room very deliberately not looking at her, Kat felt a pang of guilt. Well, she'd just have to get over that. *To whom much is given, much is expected.*

Chapter 19

Get Thee to a High School Costume
Shop on the Other Side of Town

For Jules, the days between her big fight with Kat and her birthday on Saturday couldn't pass fast enough. There were a couple of moments at school when Kat seemed like she might have wanted to talk or apologize or something, but those moments passed fairly quickly. Jules figured it would be tough to take back anything that was said by either of them, so maybe it was best she didn't say anything for a while.

But just as she was getting ready to forgive and forget, and maybe even make the first move herself, she saw Kat hanging out with those two airheaded harpies Zoe and Darcy. It positively drove her up a wall. On Thursday, they'd come wandering into Ms. Tate's class twenty minutes late with smug grins on their faces like they were getting away with something so naughty. It made Jules want to puke and immediately sent all thoughts of trying to work things out with Kat out of her head. Let her apologize first. Then, we'll see.

Instead she had her own birthday to plan. And even though Kat wasn't going to be there, this was going to be a big deal. So on Friday afternoon as Ms. Donovan had arranged, the entire Shakespeare Club piled into one of the parents' mininvans and headed to the high school. Everyone was excited about looking through the drama department's costumes to figure out what they were wearing to the Renaissance Faire.

Jules sat next to her friend Rory Retzlaff, a slightly tubby, sandy-haired boy she had a bit of a crush on because he was so funny. He always talked about how he was going to be running away to join the Renaissance Faire himself someday.

"You're so full of it!" Jules laughed at him as the van pulled out of the Willkie parking lot.

"You just wait!" said Rory. "Next year you guys will be coming to see me."

"As what? Court jester?"

"I don't know. Maybe I could be a falconer or something."

"Yeah," laughed Jules, "I hear falconry is a real growth industry, right up there with high tech."

"You laugh now, but who'll be laughing when my birds are trained to do surgical strikes against my mortal enemies?"

For a brief moment, Jules entertained a fantasy of

Rory's imaginary falcons attacking Kat and her band of Glitter Girl hangers-on. She imagined training the falcons to snatch those hideous spangled engineer's hats off their empty little heads and keep flying until they dropped them all into nearby Mirror Lake. However the fantasy abruptly ended when she thought about the possibility of exposing the innocent marine life in the lake to such toxically high levels of lameness. The environmentalist in her couldn't bear to do it, even in her mind.

In the front passenger seat of the minivan, Jules saw that Ms. Donovan was busy texting someone on her cell phone. She looked a little upset. Ms. Donovan had been a little extra moody as they were getting ready for the Faire, but Jules had just thought that was because her teacher was going to be on the hook if any of the costumes were damaged or lost. Maybe all this texting meant something else. Maybe boy trouble.

The short van ride to the high school was over quickly. Ms. Donovan stuffed her cell phone into her purse and practically barked at the students to get out. As Jules hopped out of the van with Rory, she thought she saw Ms. Donovan wipe a tear out of her eye.

"Is everything okay, Ms. Donovan?" Jules asked.

"Yes, fine," the teacher answered, wiping away a second

tear and taking a deep breath. "'Let me not think on it,'" she said, quoting from *Hamlet*. "'Frailty, thy name is woman.' Come on, kids, let's go."

Ms. Donovan turned on her heel and led the small group of students into the costume shop behind the theater. The theater department at the high school was famous for its lavish productions and had been awarded a big grant from the state a few years ago to improve the arts education in the city. So going into the costume shop was simply amazing. It was like stepping back in time. There were gorgeous turn-of-the-century dresses from last year's production of *Hello, Dolly*! And over there, the simple peasant clothes from two seasons ago when they did *Fiddler on the Roof*. But three racks down was the real treasure trove—the Shakespeare stuff. The members of the club were drawn magnetically to the costumes.

"They're just soooo beautiful!" Jules said, holding up a much-too-big taffeta gown that must have been worn by somebody royal in one of the plays. Jules was mesmerized.

"Jules what do you think?" Rory said, wandering around in a donkey's head costume from *A Midsummer Night's Dream*.

"I think you're wearing the wrong end of the donkey," Jules said.

"Ha, ha." Rory laughed and turned and nearly ran over Gwen Roswell, who was trying on some slippers that didn't quite match her gown.

"Were we born in the wrong century or what?" said Jenny Burcher, looking at the rack of clothes in front of her.

"Yeah, except for the pestilence and plague, it was a real charmer," said Jules, whose romantic streak was about a half inch deep at best.

"But they were *so* well-dressed!" said Jenny. "And the men were all so chivalrous! Putting down their cloaks so that their lady could walk across a mud puddle. Can you imagine?"

"Chivalry is dead, ladies," came Ms. Donovan's severe voice from two racks away. "Now let's make our selections so we can go."

Jenny and Jules looked at each other. Awkward!

Jules found a costume that fit her decently—a dark green costume that the character Portia wore in the *Merchant of Venice*. Jules really liked that character because she had a lot of spunk and she wasn't going to let people push her around. At one point in the play, she even disguises herself as a man so that she can plead a case in court. Her mom the lawyer would especially like that part. Anyway, the costume fit. Well, it *nearly* fit if she did some strategic stuffing in the chest area. Plus, it wasn't too frilly or girly like some of the others, so she figured it would more than do the trick for Saturday.

After another thirty minutes, everyone had pretty much settled on a costume and was ready to head back to Willkie. The group had turned positively giddy after an hour of trying on Elizabethan costumes. Even Ms. Donovan seemed to have gotten over whatever bee might have been in her bonnet. She had chosen a lovely dress that Ophelia wore in *Hamlet* before she went lovesick crazy and tossed herself in the river. Jules just had to hope her teacher's mental state was a bit better than that. This *was*, after all, the twenty-first century.

On the ride home, all the students started to sing a song they knew from Madrigals, "This Sweet Merry Month of May," even though it was the middle of October. Jules sang along for a bit and smiled:

> *This sweet and merry month of May,*
> *While Nature wantons in her prime,*
> *And birds do sing, and beasts do play*
> *For pleasure of the joyful time*

As she listened to the mostly in-tune laughing voices that filled the van, she thought that she really *didn't* need to have Kat at the Faire anyway. These were her *real* friends, weren't they? The ones who didn't let their heads get turned by something as dumb as Glitter Girl. By the end of the ride she had almost convinced herself it was true.

Almost.

Chapter 20

Uneasy Lies the Head
That Wears the Crown

Saturday. The Day. The Date. It had been circled on both Kat's and Jules's calendars (although for totally different reasons) for some time.

Kat woke that bright fall morning with a mixture of excitement, queasiness, and anticipation. It was that roller-coaster feeling again. Sort of like she felt when she had gotten the ride home from Kyle, which seemed like a lifetime ago. Kat knew that whatever happened, she would be able to divide the rest of her life into two easily defined sections: "Before Saturday" and "After Saturday." It wasn't quite Pearl Harbor Day or the adoption of the Declaration of Independence on the Fourth of July, but it was close enough for a fourteen-year-old girl in the middle of Indiana.

The launch party didn't officially begin until the afternoon, but Chelsea had called the night before and made it clear that she wanted all her Alpha Girls there no later than noon. That would give her the chance to go over what they were supposed to do and where they were supposed to stand during the show. Kat was looking forward to meeting the other girls, after hearing about them for so long. She felt sure they would hit it off right away, since they had so much in common. It would be nice to get a look at what these other Alpha Girls were like. What would an Alpha Girl from Alaska be like? From California? From Idaho? Who knew? That was part of the excitement of them all being together in one place for this big launch party.

Since TeenZone was going to carry the whole show live, there would be no retakes if she happened to win and flub up her speech. She wasn't that worried about that part. She had always done well in speech class, and while she wasn't much for reciting Shakespearean verse like Jules was, she had practiced her speech with Chelsea and her mom enough so that she'd be ready if her name were called.

Kat tossed on a pair of sweats and a T-shirt and went downstairs for breakfast. She had slept late, and she wasn't really hungry, so she just grabbed a yogurt from the fridge and left it at that. Her mom had gone to get her hair done on the off chance she'd be on camera during the show, so Kat was on her own again. She flopped on the sofa with her yogurt and watched a little TV while she ate.

Nothing that was on really sparked her interest that

morning, and it was weird to think that in a few hours' time, *she* was going to be the one on TV. She had been on TV only once before, a few years ago. It was on a local news show called *Indiana's Best Kids!* when they did a spot on the neighborhood recycling program that she and Jules had started. Well, Jules had started it mostly. But Kat had helped out and they both got to be interviewed by one of the reporters from Channel 5.

It seemed like such a long time ago, but it was only when they were in the fifth grade. Kat had a theory about years when you are a kid. They were like dog years, with one year counting for maybe seven or eight. Then when you get to high school, the years slow waaaaaaay down some more, and it's like a lifetime to get through those four years of school. Kat figured that when people got older, like thirty, things would speed up again. And by the time you get to be a senior citizen like Kat's grandparents, you would just wander around the house and wonder where all the time had gone.

Speaking of the time, Kat checked the clock over the big-screen TV in the living room. It was already 10 a.m. That gave her plenty of time to get to the school, but she knew she had one more errand to run before she went anywhere. She looked to the kitchen table, where the enormous

Shakespeare book was sitting. It was wrapped now in some special paper she had sold a few years ago as a fund-raiser when she had been in Girl Scouts. She only broke out that paper on special occasions these days, since there wasn't much of it left and it was really expensive. But there was enough at least to cover the book, and she had made one of her homemade cards to go along with it.

When she bought the book, she had hoped it would help smooth the rough waters caused by the slumber party. Well, those rough waters had turned into an all-out hurricane. She wasn't sure any book, even one with such beautiful binding and illustrations, could ever calm this kind of storm. Whether it would or not wasn't the point. The point was, she wanted to give it to Jules for her birthday.

She had looked on the Internet for a Shakespeare quote that would say just how she felt, but none of them quite seemed to fit the bill. Instead, she simply wrote:

I hope you have a happy birthday. Let's talk soon.

Kat

It wasn't much, but it was the best she could come up with in the situation.

After she finished her yogurt, she tossed the spoon into

the empty sink and grabbed the present from the table. She was hoping she could give it to Jules in person before she headed out to the Faire with her Shakespeare friends. In a way, though, she was kind of hoping she could just leave it on the steps and leave the ball in Jules's court. With so much going on, Kat wasn't sure if she was up for any more Jules drama this morning, good or bad.

As she moved toward the door, she could hear the familiar "bounce, bounce, swish" of Kyle out in the driveway working on his game. *Great*, thought Kat, *Kyle. Another big bowl full of Awkward Flakes this early in the morning*. Kat took a deep breath, wiped a few stray hairs out of her face, and then headed out the door and across the cul-de-sac.

Kyle saw her coming but didn't stop shooting the ball. His free throw clanged noisily off the rim.

"Follow-through!" he said to himself angrily.

Kat didn't quite know what to say. "Hey, Kyle," was as good as anything else she could come up with, so that is just what she said.

"Oh, hey," said Kyle, pretending to just notice her for the first time. "How's it going?"

"Okay," said Kat, uncomfortably shifting from one foot to the other. "Is Jules around? I got this birthday present for her."

"Oh uh, no. She and her friends have already gone over to Ms. Donovan's place to get into costume and practice their song and stuff."

"What about you? Are you going to the Faire?"

"Oh, we kinda had a family party here last night. Doublets and sonnets aren't really my thing."

"Yeah, mine either," Kat said, grateful to have something they could agree on.

She took a deep breath. After all the weirdness at school the last time she saw him, she knew she just had to say something to Kyle. *Something.*

"I guess you heard Jules and I had a fight."

Kyle paused for a moment before he took his next shot. "Yeah, maybe I did." The ball flew awkwardly out of his hand and missed the basket altogether. Air ball. It bounced down the inclined driveway and stopped right at Kat's feet. She picked up the ball and gave it her best girl throw back to him. It wasn't much of a toss and Kyle had to lunge to his right to catch it. He shot the ball again.

"You know, I saw what you said about Jules on that video. She's right to be mad at you. I'd be mad at you too."

Kat was embarrassed but tried not to let it show. "I can't believe she showed you that."

"She didn't have to. In fact, I'm sure she never would. But it's all over the Internet now. It's got like 30,000 hits already."

Kat couldn't believe it. So 30,000 people, 30,000 *strangers* had already watched what she had said on her porch a few nights ago? It was too unreal. Her head was spinning. For a fleeting instant, she wondered if it would hurt her chances to be chosen the next Glitter Girl. But then she thought about Jules and how positively *mortified* she would be if she knew people were watching her and laughing at what Kat had said about her.

"Look," said Kyle, "I know Jules is different. She's not like your other friends. But she's a good kid. In fact, don't tell her this, but she's probably the best kid I know. And I think you know that too. And she would never give her friendship to someone who doesn't deserve it."

"So what are you saying?"

"I'm saying you need to start deserving it again."

Kat didn't know what to say. She just stood with her arms folded around the massive book, watching Kyle shoot the ball. She breathed deeply.

"Well, anyway," she said, "can you give this to Jules for me?"

She held out the book, but Kyle didn't even look at her.

"Just put it in the backseat of the Mustang. We're all going out for dinner when they get back. I'll give it to her then."

"Okay," she said, not knowing what else to say. She walked to the edge of the driveway, and opened the car door, laying the book on the empty seat. Kyle didn't say anything more after she had done that, so Kat was left with nothing to do but make an awkward retreat back to her house. When she got to the bottom of the driveway, Kyle finally stopped shooting the ball for a moment.

"Hey, Kat," he said.

Kat turned quickly.

"I hope you win today."

"What?"

"The Glitter Girl thing. I hope you get it. I know it's important to you."

"Thanks," said Kat. But as she turned to walk toward the house, she wondered if she really should have thanked Kyle. Was he really being sincere? Or was he taking a jab at her and her priorities? Suggesting that Glitter Girl was more important to her than her friendship with Jules. She turned back to look at Kyle, hoping something in his expression or the way he was shooting the ball would let her know if he was being sarcastic. But he was gone.

What wasn't gone was the bad feeling that was bubbling

up inside Kat. Was it guilt? Insecurity? Shame? *Ooooh. Darn that Kyle.* She wished she'd never gone over to begin with. She stomped up the steps into her house and slammed the door.

Chapter 21

To Thine Own Self Be True

"OMG! This is the most sick, swaggiest, hardcore partay evah!" shouted Zoe, throwing out all the slang she could manage in one breath.

"Yeah, it's like totally eviscerated!" agreed Darcy who had read that word in a book somewhere and thought it sounded cool. The fact that in reality it meant the act of removing the intestines of an animal was unimportant to her. Just as everything else was at that moment except the magnificently organized chaos around her.

"Kat, don't you think this is totally off the chain?" Zoe asked rhetorically because she was sure Kat absolutely did think so. How could she not?

Truth was, standing there in the backstage area of the Glitter Girl launch party, Kat should have been waaaaay more excited than she was. After all, the junior high gym had been positively transformed. The job that had been half underway when they snuck into the gym on Thursday was now complete, and no expense had been spared. A comedian was on stage right now, warming up the crowd before the live show started on TeenZone in a few minutes.

Yep, Kat had every reason to be excited. But her encounter with Kyle in the driveway a few hours earlier kept nagging at her and left her seriously bummed out as she peeked out of a break in a huge black curtain that she and the other Alpha Girls were hidden behind. It didn't help that all the other Alpha Girls seemed to be so into winning that nobody was speaking to each other.

Beyond the curtain, there were millions of sparkling lights, a shiny leopard-print floor, and a huge mirrored stage with a backdrop of thousands of bright pink bulbs that flashed the words "Glitter Girl" in ten-foot-high letters. As the comedian left the stage to the applause of the gathered throng, the house band tore into some earsplitting music. Its bass was turned up so loud that Kat could actually feel her internal organs vibrate to the rhythm.

A whole section in the middle of the gym floor was roped off to make room for a platform with a giant mixing board and the biggest video cameras Kat had ever laid eyes on. There was a crew of fifteen guys in black, wearing headsets and all running frantically around. One of them was operating a camera suspended on a big, black pole that could swing freely back and forth over the heads of the audience in front of the stage. In fact, Kat could see the images it was capturing on the *ginormous* hi-def monitors that hung on either side of the stage.

"OMG squared! That was Gomez Endicott!" Zoe jumped up and down as the celebrity blogger's face flashed across the screen, pores and all. "I can't believe Chelsea pulled off getting him here!"

Kat wasn't surprised. After all, Chelsea reminded her a lot of those super wedding planners on TV, with her smartphones and Bluetooth and organizer and the nice way she seemed to order everyone around. Kat didn't think there was a whole lot that Chelsea couldn't pull off. Although she *was* surprised Chelsea had somehow managed to get rid of the cheesy, sweaty stench of B.O. that hit you whenever you walked into the gym. Kudos for that at least, Chelsea!

"Look at all those people!" shouted Kat's mother, coming up behind her and giving her an air kiss on the side of her cheek to avoid messing up Kat's makeup. Or maybe she was avoiding messing up hers. Kat couldn't be sure. "And they're all here to see you!"

"Not just me, Mom," Kat said, pointing to the other forty-nine potential "Glitter Girls" who were anxiously milling around backstage. Like Kat, they were all sporting various Glitter Girl looks. And at least six of them were wearing that same stupid engineer's cap she had on. Kat wasn't going to wear it, but Chelsea insisted. In fact, she practically demanded it. It was almost as if she was trying to make some sort of point. Kat peeked out at the sea of girls crowding the gymnasium who'd come for the launch. Hundreds and hundreds of them. And they were dressed just like her too.

Or am I dressed like them? It was a troubling thought that led Kat to remember what Jules had said to her about selling out and losing her sense of herself. Which in turn led Kat to think about Jules and the birthday party Kat wasn't at, and what Jules was doing at that very moment. And all that led inevitably to a sudden, guilty lurch in the pit of Kat's stomach.

* * *

"*Huzzah!*"

The two o'clock joust had just ended and Sir Roderick, he of the black and gold colors, had come out the victor. Which was cool because Jules and her party of birthday revelers happened to be sitting in his section and therefore he was their knight to root for. Jules looked down the benches and could see the cheering faces of those who had come to celebrate the anniversary of her birth. And it was a darn good turnout. All her Shakespeare and Math Club friends were there, as was Ms. Donovan, who looked great in the Ophelia costume she'd gotten from the high school. Jules thought it was cool of her to come, considering that she was a teacher and already had given up most of the hours in her week to be with her students. She certainly wasn't obligated to spend her Saturday with them too. Of course, she would have been at the Faire anyway, given that she volunteered every season, and Jules got the sense it was the highlight of her year.

Naturally Jules's parents were there because, well, they were her parents and *were* obligated. Although her dad had actually gotten into the spirit of the day by putting on a colorful jester's hat and talking in a weird accent that was more leprechaun than anything remotely British. But everyone in their group thought it was hysterically funny and kept egging him on. Normally, Jules would have thought it was funny too, but she simply wasn't feeling too festive at the moment. Yeah, she was excited to turn fourteen. And yeah, she was celebrating with her friends and family in her absolute favorite place on Earth.

But she wasn't exactly sure why she was having trouble laughing at her dad's goofiness. Or why she couldn't muster an appetite for the giant Tofurkey leg she'd bought at Ye Vegan Vestibule. She had been carrying the oversized hunk of protein around for the last half hour, despite the fact that she hadn't yet had lunch. She convinced herself that her lack of appetite and enthusiasm had nothing to do with Kat not being there.

In fact, she had convinced herself it was *better* that Kat wasn't there, because then she'd be worried the whole time whether Kat would be bored. And she'd feel obligated to stick by Kat's side instead of enjoying her own self (which she wasn't doing anyway). Yep. She'd convinced herself 100 percent absolutely that the reason she was feeling so bummed had nothing to do with Kat.

But then when she was over playing a ring-tossing game called quoits at one of the booths, her heart lurched because she could have sworn she saw Kat outside the Pendragon Costumes tent. But when the girl turned around, she was much too short and her hair had too many highlights to be Kat. Jules felt a wave of disappointment when she realized that yes, the fact that Kat chose Glitter Girl over her party was bothering her a load more than she was admitting to herself. It was stupid to even think for an instant that Kat would miraculously show up. That only happened in movies and books. Not in life.

Jules blinked back the tears as Audrey Turner from Math Club grabbed her by her Tofurkey-clutching hand

and pulled her over to look at some pewter dragons on sale at one of the vendor booths. And as Audrey "oohed" and "ahhed" over the fine craftsmanship of the pieces, Jules pretended to care.

• • •

Don't wanna study. Don't wanna sleep.
Wanna party, party wild, party free and deep.
Platform shoes, designer clothes,
I'ma text and tweet tweet tweet
Cuz I'm livin' large, I'm livin' in charge,
I'm livin' the teen dream! Sweet!

Jessica Aguirre sang to a screaming audience of teen girls as she paraded in her metallic boots across the mirrored stage. She was wearing the teeniest belly shirt and the shortest short shorts allowed by law. Her hair was wild and her eyes were completely encircled in kohl-black makeup. And she was really good. Well, Kat assumed that she was good. Her voice was being filtered through an auto-tuner, and by the time it came out of the speakers, it sounded about as much like a human female voice as R2-D2 from *Star Wars*.

But the beat was infectious, and Kat couldn't help but

get caught up in the moment, clapping and dancing along with the crowd. And forgetting all about the sameness of everyone around her.

"All right, ladies, get ready. The big moment is at hand."

It was Chelsea, who had been running around in cool control, shouting orders and double- and triple-checking absolutely everything.

"I want all fifty of my Glitter Girls lined up alphabetically by state like I showed you at rehearsal. As soon as Jessica finishes her number, you'll walk out onstage and take your marks. Then I'll be announcing *the winner*. Now, I know you all have excellent acceptance speeches because, well, I wrote them. But just remember if you get called, a Glitter Girl carries herself with poise and elegance above all others—er, I mean, else. Above all else."

Kat felt a pang of nervousness and excitement because she could have sworn when Chelsea had said "the winner" she looked directly at Kat. Could it be possible? Or was it just her imagination?

"It's you!" said Zoe, grabbing her arm hard and whispering in her ear. "You're going to win! Did you see that? She looked right at you when she said 'the winner'! OMG cubed! My BFF is going to be the Face of Glitter Girl! And to think you almost didn't come! Good thing I got

Jules out of the picture or you would have missed the most awesomest opportunity of your life."

It took a moment, but then Kat's excitement began to fade as Zoe's words slowly sunk in.

"What did you say?" Kat asked.

"You're going to win!" repeated Zoe.

"No. The part about you getting Jules out of the picture."

Suddenly realizing she'd said too much, Zoe's eyes went wide. Kind of like a deer caught in the headlights of an eighteen-wheeler bearing down at 100 miles per hour.

"Uh, well…" Zoe stammered.

Jessica ended her song to deafening cheers and Chelsea took the stage. But Kat was only vaguely aware. Her attention was on Zoe.

"Don't be mad, okay? But I was the one who sent the video to Jules. But we did it for your own good!" she added quickly.

"We? Darcy was in on this too?"

"Puh-lease. As if."

They looked over at Darcy who was staring at a garbage can that read "WASTE PLEASE" and looking really confused.

"Then who?" demanded Kat.

Kat saw Zoe's eyes flick onto the stage and at Chelsea.

She was introducing Gregory Remoulet to a nice round of applause from the audience. Kat looked back at Zoe.

"Chelsea was in on it?" asked Kat, feeling completely blindsided.

"Yeah. She's the one who took the video."

"*What?*"

"But she did it for your own good. She told me so! She took me out for some shopping and we had a talk about your future. And she said how Jules was going to ruin everything for you, and did I want that? And of course I said no. And then she gave me the video and told me what to do. And we agreed that it was for the best."

"Psst! Move it!"

Kat turned to look behind her. It was the girl from Iowa giving her a shove toward the stage. Kat realized many of the Glitter Girl hopefuls were already out onstage and she was holding up the rest of the line.

Not knowing what else to do, Kat walked out and took her place, with the pushy girl from Iowa on her heels. Chelsea shot an irritated look at the two of them for causing the delay. The girl from Iowa whispered angrily, "You better not have ruined this for me!"

But Kat wasn't even listening. She was still in shock over what she had just learned.

So Chelsea Ambrose was the one behind her fallout with Jules. She actually planned it! She knew Chelsea was single-minded, but Kat had never imagined she would stoop so low as to ruin a friendship. And in such a mean and sneaky way. Showing up at the school and taking her on that shopping trip and pretending to care. She'd deliberately set Kat up and deliberately made Kat hurt a totally trusting and caring human being. Her best friend, in fact, who had never done anything underhanded or nasty in their entire friendship.

The lights dimmed and four or five brilliant spotlights scanned the girls as dramatic music played in the background to build up the suspense. Chelsea was still at the microphone. Kat focused on her. While the other girls were feeling excitement and anticipation, all she could feel was hurt and betrayal. She stared daggers at Chelsea as she went on with her speech.

But Kat realized it wasn't just Chelsea that she was mad at. After all, it *was* Chelsea's job to make sure the whole Glitter Girl thing went smoothly. That's what was important to her. How could Kat expect her to care about anything else? Anyway, she didn't even really know Kat, except as the girl who delivered big sales, the Alpha Girl.

And Kat had let herself get totally caught up in it. For

what? Popularity? Fame? Sure that all sounded exciting. But what was the cost? Not only did she lose her best friend, but she had also lost a sense of herself and who she was. Kat suddenly felt really angry. Not at Chelsea and not at Zoe. But at herself, for losing sight of what was important.

Chelsea had arrived at the big moment. With a dramatic flourish, she opened one of those fancy envelopes like they have at the Academy Awards and said, "And the winner of the all-expenses-paid trip to New York, where she will participate in a photo shoot that will make her the Face of Glitter Girl is…Kat Connors from right here in Indiana!"

The crowd erupted in cheers.

Kat blinked as if in a dream. She could have sworn she'd heard her name called. She looked in the wings and saw Zoe and Darcy hugging and jumping in unison. She saw her mom crying big sloppy tears of joy and giving her a thumbs-up. She looked up at the Jumbotrons and saw them filled with her surprised face. She turned and saw Chelsea looking very pleased and waving for her to come forward. And she knew…she had won.

Kat stood frozen. It wasn't until Iowa gave her a nudge that she staggered forward to center stage. Chelsea met her halfway, took her by the elbow, and leaned in to whisper. Kat thought it was to congratulate her.

"Straighten the hat. And don't stray from the speech we practiced. And remember, in 'Remoulet,' the 't' is silent."

Chelsea had managed the whole little speech through a big smile and clenched teeth. Her mouth hadn't moved at all. And when she guided Kat to the microphone, she let go and stepped to the side, the big smile still in place.

Kat stood there blinking. As the applause began to die down, she stared out into the audience. It took a moment for her eyes to adjust because of the bright lights, and then she could see them...hundreds of young faces all staring up at her. Excited faces, wishful faces, even some jealous faces. Faces of girls who would have given anything to be in Kat's shoes. Faces that all wished they could be Kat. Yet at that moment Kat wished very much that *she* wasn't Kat.

As she scanned the sea of girls before her, Kat caught a glimpse of one girl in the front row wearing the very same bracelets she was wearing. Another wore the same bedazzled vest. And the engineer's hat. There were dozens of them, all over the auditorium. And that's when she realized it.

I'm NOT me. Not anymore. I'm exactly like everybody else.

"Miss Connors?" Mr. Remoulet leaned over to her. "You have a few words, I understand?"

Kat stepped up to the microphone and pulled out the

prepared speech. She looked at it for a moment and then put it away.

"When I was first contacted by Glitter Girl, I was so excited. I mean, who wouldn't be? Getting picked for your taste and for being a girl that other girls look to and admire. How cool is that? I mean, it's something we all really desperately want, right? To be accepted. To fit in."

There was a murmur of agreement from the audience. Kat took a quick glance over at Chelsea and saw a concerned look flash across her face. Kat swallowed hard and continued.

"And I totally thought the Glitter Girl stuff was the coolest stuff. For the coolest girls. And they do have some cool stuff. I mean, those skinny jeans with the tiny pockets are *to die for*."

The audience applauded and cheered appreciatively. Chelsea relaxed a little. Kat was going off book and throwing some of her own stuff in there, but hey, the audience was responding.

"But there is nothing cool about turning your back on your friends. It's gross to admit, but I did that recently. I'm not even kidding. I acted like a total jerk to my best friend. All because she didn't fit in with what I thought was cool… with all of this." Kat indicated herself, her whole look.

Out of the corner of her eye, Kat saw Chelsea's smile turn to a snarl and Mr. Remoulet looking very unhappy indeed. There was no turning back now.

"I mean, look at us. There's nothing unique or individual about us. We all look the same. We act the same. And if anyone is different, we treat them like they don't belong. Is that cool? No. But I did that to somebody just because she had the guts to be herself. And the crazy thing is, that's why I liked her in the first place!"

Kat held out her wrist, showing her bracelets to the crowd. "This, this is just…stuff. It doesn't mean anything. Friendship is what matters. Loyalty is what matters. Being brave enough to be yourself is what matters. Because of Glitter Girl, I let myself get turned into a mannequin," she said repeating Jules's words from their fight. "Brainless and heartless and made of plastic."

There was an audible gasp from the crowd. Kat had to hand it to Jules. She could come up with some real zingers when she was mad.

"I'm sorry, Mr. Remoulet. I appreciate that you picked me. But I'm definitely not the Face of Glitter Girl. I'm just the face of plain old me. Oh, and Chelsea, before someone sends you a secret video of me saying it—this hat is stupid!"

Kat pulled off the engineer's cap and threw it at Chelsea, who fumbled as she caught it. Then Kat walked off stage.

Everyone in the auditorium stood in stunned silence. Nobody knew what to do. For once in her life, even Chelsea was speechless. But Chelsea being Chelsea quickly composed herself. She put on the engineer's cap and her biggest, fakest smile to date, then grabbed the microphone and shouted, "Free lip gloss for everyone!"

Chelsea gave a signal and stagehands began shooting packages of lip gloss out of a gigantic cannon into the audience.

The band cranked up another jam and the audience erupted in cheers, immediately forgetting what had happened onstage seconds before.

Chapter 22

Neither a Borrower Nor a Lender Be
(Unless You're in a Really Big Hurry)

Once she got off the stage, Kat ran. She pushed past several stagehands and headed toward the locker rooms. By the time she had made it to the door, she heard the announcement that the nasty Alpha Girl from Iowa had already been chosen as a replacement for her. And the house band welcomed her to center stage with the same blaring music that had greeted Kat five minutes earlier. Clearly, Chelsea Ambrose had barely missed a beat. She was going to land on her feet on this one, Kat could tell already.

Kat moved quickly through the locker room, pushed open the disarmed fire door, and stepped into the bright October day. The Earth seemed to be spinning extra slowly as she took a deep breath of the air around her. The fall colors were just starting in Indiana, and everywhere she looked were the brilliant reds and yellows of the leaves on the trees. She had never really noticed how beautiful the grounds of the school were until this very moment. She had to catch her breath; the colors were overwhelming to her.

Kat knew she had to talk to Jules as soon as possible. She had to tell her what happened, leaving nothing out. There was a shuttle bus that picked up people going to the Renaissance Faire right in front of Willkie every half hour. She looked down at her Glitter Girl watch. Just two minutes and the bus would be there. Jules was supposed to sing her solo at three. If Kat made this bus, she just might be able to catch Jules's performance. She quickly ran over the small hill that led from the gym to the bus stop, almost falling a couple of times because she was moving so fast.

She was out of breath when she arrived at the bus stop. Two elderly couples with a picnic basket were already there waiting, as was a teenage boy in green tights and a Robin Hood hat. Kat couldn't sit down. Instead she paced back and forth, looking down the street for the shuttle bus. That is, until she heard—

"Kat!" She turned around and saw her mom heading down the hill toward her. Ugh. Thrilling getaways are always easier when you don't get a ride from your mom in the first place. Kat braced herself. She knew she had disappointed her mom. She knew she had an earful coming, but she didn't care. She'd take whatever her mom had to dish out. It was a small price to pay to get out of there.

Her mom came right up to her just as the low-pitched

rumble of the shuttle-bus engine could be heard in the distance.

"What were you thinking making a speech like that?" Trudy looked at Kat like she was crazy.

Kat answered, looking at the ground. "Not quite like we rehearsed it, was it?"

"That's for sure," Trudy responded. "Do you know what you just did in there? Do you have any idea? You said no to a huge opportunity. To a lot of stuff!"

"So what?" snapped Kat. "Look at all the stuff you've got, Mom. Are *you* happy? Does it make up for the fact that Dad 'chooses' to be at his job instead of with us? Cuz that's what he does, you know. He told me himself. And you 'choose' to let it happen. And then you let yourself be bought off. Well, I don't want to do that. I choose not to!"

Kat was surprised by her own outburst. But it felt good to say it. What didn't feel good was the hurt look in her mom's eyes.

"I'm sorry, Mom. I—" started Kat.

"No, it's okay," Trudy stopped her. "It sounds like you know what you want."

Kat shrugged. "Not really. I just know I need to get out to the Faire and see Jules."

Trudy looked at her daughter for a moment and nodded. "Then let's get you to the Faire and see Jules. Come on, we'll take my car."

Kat's mom put her arm around her as they headed to the parking lot. As they did, the shuttle bus stopped and picked up the remaining customers and started out on the ten-minute drive to the fairgrounds just outside of town. It didn't matter, though. In a few minutes Kat would be—

"Aiiiiiiigh!" Kat screamed, arriving at her mom's Range Rover. The car was *totally* boxed in. There were so many cars in the parking lot, and they had been there so early that there was no way Kat's mom could get their vehicle out of that parking lot without magic tricks or dynamite.

Kat looked helplessly at the car and then back at the shuttle bus as it disappeared into the distance.

"Now what?" she said, almost crying to her mom.

VROOOM!

Almost in answer to her question, a vintage Ford Mustang came roaring over the hill toward the parking lot. Kyle! Here at school! By himself! What in the world?

SCREECH! The car skidded to a halt right in front of Kat. When Kyle put on the brakes, the car fishtailed a bit and almost hit a blue Volkswagen, but Kat didn't even notice. It could have sideswiped a whole line of cars for all she cared. Kyle was here. But how?

"Kyle? What are you doing here?"

Kyle hopped out of the car. "I just saw the whole thing on TV. Are you okay? They cut to a commercial before you could finish and then you were gone."

"Never mind about that. Can you get us out to the fairgrounds?"

"Uh, yeah, I guess I can find it. I've never driven out there before."

"I'll show you the way!" Kat's mom yelled, hopping in the backseat. "Come on, Kyle, put this bad boy in gear!"

Kat and Kyle looked at each other. This day was getting more ridiculous by the minute. Kyle quickly opened the door for Kat and she hopped in, smiling. Who said chivalry was dead? Kyle slammed the door closed and raced back to the driver's side. He slammed his own door. They all put their seat belts on and Kyle awkwardly put the car in gear.

"Take 34th Street to the highway!" Trudy barked from the backseat. "Waveland is totally jammed at this time of day!"

Neither Kyle nor Kat was about to argue, and the Mustang sped off into the warm Indiana afternoon, disappearing over a hill at a speed that Kyle's driver's ed teacher would *not* have approved of.

The Faire was five miles away. Jules's big solo was in eight minutes.

Chapter 23

Friendship Is Constant in All Things

"*Left!* Turn left right here!" came the voice from the back of the Mustang. Kyle's car veered dangerously close to the edge of the country road but managed to maneuver the turn without the car doing one of those 360 spins that only seem to happen in the movies. As Kat gripped the dashboard for dear life, it seemed very much like a movie to her. Everything was spinning around her double-time now, and Kyle's driving was exhilarating and downright scary at the same time. And Kat's mom? Barking instructions from the back of the Mustang? Too bizarre for words.

The Mustang barreled over a small hill, and all four wheels might have even left the ground for a moment as the car sped past a sign pointing to the "Renaissance Faire—1/4 mile." Kat looked at her watch. Five minutes to three. They were almost there. Kat breathed deeply. Until—

Squawk! Cluck! Grumble! Grumble!

As they came over the hill, Kyle had to put on the brakes in a major hurry. A horse-drawn cart carrying a load of funny-looking chickens was stopped in the middle of the narrow roadway. A few of the crates of chickens had fallen off the back of the cart as it went over the hill, and the crates had shattered. Now, the hens and roosters were strutting about all over the road as if they owned the place. A man in a peasant costume scurried about trying to round them up and get them back on the cart. Kat looked at the spectacle in disbelief. The sixteenth century could be sooooo inconvenient sometimes!

Kyle looked at the road in front of him. He knew they would never make if they had to wait for Old MacDonald up there to collect all his runaway birds.

"Go!" said Kyle.

"What?"

"You're going to miss it! Let me worry about the car."

Kat looked at her watch. Two minutes to go.

"Go on!" said her mom. "We'll catch up to you later."

Kat scrambled out of the car and ran down the road, avoiding the chicken catastrophe as best she could.

She was about ten yards from the Mustang when she heard Kyle's voice behind her.

"Wait!" he said, running behind her and dodging chickens all the while.

Kat stopped.

"You forgot this!" Kyle said, holding out the Shakespeare book that Kat had left in the car earlier.

Kyle smiled. "It's not a birthday without a present, is it?"

Impulsively, and without even thinking about it, she gave Kyle a quick kiss on the lips and sprinted down the road toward the entrance to the Faire, now in sight at the bottom of the hill.

Kat arrived out of breath, quickly paid her entrance fee, and dashed into the Faire. She ran past a couple of roving magicians and a guy who for some reason was making a sandwich with his feet and headed toward the big crowds that were near the jousting arena. She heard a cheer go up from the arena and feared she might be too late. Jules was only the warm-up act for the three o'clock joust. They couldn't be doing all that cheering for her, could they?

Kat got to the crowded arena area and elbowed her way toward the front. She didn't have to push too hard. In spite of the swordplay and poor table manners, the Renaissance Faire crowd was actually a fairly orderly bunch, and they parted easily when given a reason to move. After a few seconds, Kat had worked her way to the front of the crowd. She looked around but couldn't see Jules at all. Was she really too late?

Then, from one end of the arena, all the familiar faces

from Willkie came marching in, led by Ms. Donovan. They were introduced by the announcer at the joust in very flowery language: "Having journeyed to us all the way from the hamlet of Carmel." Kat suddenly found herself being jostled around as a very fat man in a monk's outfit pushed his way to the front. She strained to see around him as the group took their spots on the opposite side of the arena.

She saw Ms. Donovan, looking very at home in her Renaissance garb, and then Rory Retzlaff, carrying a guitar and waving to friends in the crowd. Then came April Wong, Dylan O'Brien, and a couple of kids Kat didn't know. Finally, coming out last was Jules. She looked glum and nervous, as if she were actually going to be hanged from the fake gallows that stood in the back of the arena, rather than sing a solo to warm up the crowd.

Ms. Donovan stepped to the front and curtsied extravagantly to the crowd. Then she turned around and held her hands up to begin conducting the group. Rory started to strum his guitar, and the other singers began to hum quietly. Jules stepped to the front of the group; she took a deep breath and began to sing:

Alas, my love, you do me wrong,
To cast me off discourteously.

For I have loved you well and long,
Delighting in your company.

Even Kat could recognize the melody. It was "Greensleeves," one of the most famous songs from the Renaissance. Jules's voice was just so pretty and sad and pure. So different from Jessica Aguirre and her auto-tuned robot pop that Kat had just escaped from. She caught Jules's eye. There was a little catch in Jules's voice as she noticed Kat, looking right at her. She stared at her friend so intently that Kat was afraid Jules would lose her place in the song. But, instead, as the rest of the chorus joined in, Jules's voice grew stronger, almost as if she was getting her strength from seeing her friend. And truth be told, she was. As Jules wrapped up the final verse of her solo, Kat smiled through her tears.

Then, Jules smiled. Pretty soon, Kat could see that Jules was crying too. As the song ended, Kat and Jules just kept looking at each other, neither quite believing what was happening. It seemed like all the other noises of the Faire disappeared. Suddenly, the weird silence was broken.

"Kat!" Jules screamed out.

"Jules!" Kat yelled. She crawled under the restraining rope and ran into the arena. Jules ran to greet her. They met at the center of the arena.

"But, I…what about Glitter Girl?" asked Jules.

"Some things are more important," replied Kat, meaning it with all her heart.

Then they hugged. Just hugged. Long and hard. They didn't say anything for a long time, but each was thinking the same thing. *Finally.* Even though nobody else knew what all the hugging was about, loud cheers and "Huzzahs!" went up all around the arena. Even some of the knights and ladies-in-waiting came out from the back of the arena to watch what was going on and clap along.

Jules and Kat finally broke the hug. For the first time, Jules noticed Kat was still in her full Glitter Girl clothes and makeup.

"You look ridiculous," Jules said, wiping away a tear.

"So do you," Kat smiled and sniffled.

Then, Jules took Kat's hand. "Come on," she said. "Let me show you around."

Chapter 24

All's Well That Ends Well

"It's so big!" said Jules, admiring the wrapped gift on her lap. The girls had moved away from the jousting arena and sat in the shade of a large oak tree.

"Open it!" said Kat smiling brightly.

Jules did as she was told, starting in one corner. As the paper began to fall away, she glimpsed the beautiful, gold-leafed pages. Excited, she tore the paper completely off, revealing the treasure that was beneath it. She gasped!

"Wow, Kat..." Jules said paging through the book. "This must have cost you a fortune."

"It's nice, isn't it?"

"It's more than nice," Jules said, smiling widely. "It's perfect."

The two girls hugged again.

As they broke the hug, Jules and Kat looked across the field and saw a group of college kids hanging out together. They were laughing and watching some of the performers get soaked at the "Dunk a Wench" tank near the center of the Faire. Girls in costumes clung on to a thick rope at the end of a giant pulley and were repeatedly dropped into a huge wooden vat of water. Then they were yanked back out a few seconds later, soaking wet and greeted by the cheers and howls of the crowd. Kat and Jules laughed along with them.

"Do you think we'll still be friends when we're in college?" Jules asked, suddenly serious.

Kat thought about it for a second. The easy answer was to say, "Of course. You'll be my friend forever. That's what BFF means, after all." But she didn't say that. Everything that had happened in the last few weeks wouldn't let her say that. Instead, she took Jules's hand and said, "I don't know. But I know you're my friend now. And that's what matters."

Jules smiled. Somehow that answer made more sense than anything else Kat could have said. The two friends walked through the Faire arm in arm. And somehow that was good enough too.

. . .

The girls spent the rest of the afternoon together at the Faire. Laughing, talking, trying all of the weird medieval food, or at least all the food Jules could eat with a clear conscience. The more Kat got to know Jules's friends from the Shakespeare Club and the Math Club, the more she liked them. These kids who Kat would *never* have thought to invite to that Glitter Girl slumber party, an event that now seemed as far away as the Crusades. Rory Retzlaff really *was* a funny kid, and Kat smiled at how he and Jules would kid each other and flirt in their semi-dorky way. It was fun, and not once did Kat think about how she looked.

Jules's parents went shopping on their own for pewter and silver craftwork, but Ms. Donovan hung out with the Willkie kids for a while after their performance. She seemed very much at home among the lords and ladies at the Faire. Kat knew she had some unfinished business to take care of with her. Since Jules was watching Rory play an old-time dice game called Farkle and joining in with the cheers when he made a good roll, Kat figured now was as good a time as any to talk to the teacher.

"Ms. Donovan…" she said haltingly.

"Kat!" said Ms. Donovan, turning and smiling. "Thanks for coming! We certainly didn't expect to see you here today."

"I guess I didn't expect it myself," she said. She took a deep breath and continued. "I just wanted to say that you were right about Glitter Girl. I shouldn't have let myself go so crazy about it."

"Well," said her teacher, "As Portia found out in *The Merchant of Venice*, 'All that glistens is not gold,' but I don't have to tell you that. I think you've learned that lesson pretty well."

Kat looked from Ms. Donovan to Jules, laughing and clapping next to Rory at the Farkle booth.

"Yeah," she said, "I guess I have. I feel so stupid, though."

"We all let our emotions get the better of us sometimes. We get too soon old and too late smart."

"Is that from Shakespeare too?"

"No, that's my grandma."

Jules peeled herself away from the Farkle game and rejoined Kat and Ms. Donovan. "Oh man, Rory is going to be in debt until the next century if he keeps playing like that!" She laughed. "I guess he'll have to be an indentured servant or something."

Ms. Donovan smiled, "Serfdom might be a good career choice for him. By the way, Kat," she continued, "thanks for the heads-up about Coach Scofield. I got your text about what you heard him say about me. I confronted him about it. You were right; he was a jerk. Anyway, we finally broke up last night, or to put a finer point on it, I should say that *I* broke up with *him*."

Jules turned to Kat, remembering the text that Ms.

Donovan had received on the way to the high school. "That was you?" she asked, surprised.

"I had to do something after the mean things he said…a little late, though. I should never have tried to play matchmaker with you two in the first place."

"It's not your fault. I'm a grown woman. I'm perfectly capable of making my own irresponsible decisions. At least I got a new hairstyle out of the deal. And who knows where that might lead."

Saying that, she was approached by Sir Roderick, the knight that they had been cheering earlier. He was tall, dark, and dreamy, in a King Arthur kind of way. He held out his hand to Ms. Donovan.

"Now if you'll excuse me," she said, smiling. "I have an appointment to cheer someone on at the archery exhibition." She took Sir Roderick's hand and the two disappeared into the crowd. Jules joined Kat as she watched them go, amazed.

"Huzzah indeed!" said Kat, and then she and Jules burst out laughing.

• • •

Kyle finally caught up to them a little bit after that. He had actually stopped to help the farmer collect his chickens, and it had taken longer than expected to get the wagon (and his Mustang) moving again. Apparently, a spangled

English rooster had been particularly elusive, and Kyle had to use all of his defensive skills from the basketball court to finally corral the pesky fowl.

Jules needed a few assurances that the rooster in question was being treated humanely and in compliance with international law. But Kyle was able to get out of the entire conversation by stuffing his mouth full of kettle corn as he talked, completely grossing out his younger sister and making the entire Willkie group crack up as well. Nothing like food flying from a teenager's mouth for entertainment.

• • •

It was a good hour before Kat was able to talk to her mom. It wasn't that Trudy was trying to avoid the girls, but instead she sat quietly on a bench in the shade of a giant oak tree and spoke on her cell phone the whole time. Kat could only assume she was talking long-distance to her dad, but she couldn't quite tell how the conversation was going. Finally, Trudy hung up the phone and Kat approached her.

"Is everything okay?" she asked, sitting next to her mom.

Trudy smiled and put her arm around her daughter, feeling twelve different emotions at once.

"It's going to be," she said simply. "It's going to be."

Kat wasn't quite sure what that meant, but she knew that it was true. It *was* going to be okay.

Chapter 25

What's Past Is Prologue

"Okay. Now *that's* what I'm talkin' about!" said Kat as she reached into the big bowl on her lap and grabbed a handful of popcorn and stuffed it into her mouth.

When Jules had suggested they get a Shakespeare movie for their Friday movie night, Kat agreed but insisted on picking it out. She knew exactly what she wanted to get. It wasn't one of those costume dramas with a bunch of "thees" and "thous" and stolen glances and daggers. No siree. It was about a modern-day girl who goes to Verona and finds this letter that a brokenhearted woman wrote to Juliet, the one from the Shakespeare play, like fifty years ago. Then she goes on a road trip to reunite the woman with her long-lost love. Lots of stuff happens, but basically the whole movie is an excuse for romance and lots of fabulous scenery, and Kat was a real fan of both.

The movie had just come to an end and the credits were rolling.

"You realize this wasn't really Shakespeare," said Jules,

turning off the movie and grabbing her own handful of popcorn from the bowl.

"Yeah. But you've got to admit, it was good!"

"Yeah. It was pretty good," admitted Jules, grudgingly.

"It was okay. But it could have used some swordplay," offered Rory, who was sitting on the floor at Jules's feet. This had become his regular spot ever since Jules had invited him to movie night two weeks before. She had to admit, she did like having him there. Especially when he would reach into the popcorn bowl at the same time as her and their hands would touch—which was what was happening at that exact moment! Jules blushed.

"How about you? Did you like it?" Kat offered the bowl of popcorn to Kyle, who was sitting "boyfriend" close to her, his knee touching hers.

"I refuse to answer on the grounds it may incriminate me," said Kyle, grabbing the remote from Jules and skimming channels.

Kat playfully threw a handful of popcorn at him, some of which he caught in his mouth. Kat giggled.

Jules looked away as Kyle took Kat's hand. Even though she had accepted that her best friend and brother were going out, it didn't mean she was a fan of their PDA.

"Hey, you cut off your nails," commented Kyle, noticing

that Kat no longer sported the long manicured nails that had been one of her trademarks.

"Yeah. Long nails and volunteering for Habitat for Humanity don't exactly go hand in hand. No pun intended," said Kat.

"It's a good look for you," said Kyle as he stared dreamily into her eyes.

Ew. Jules couldn't take it.

"Uh, Mrs. Connors! Can you please bring me a barf bag! I think I'm going to be sick!" yelled Jules over her shoulder.

Just then Trudy came in, dressed to the nines in a little black dress and high heels. She was putting on pearl earrings.

"What's that, dear?" she asked.

"Nothing, Mom. Jules was kidding," responded Kat. "You look really nice."

"Yeah, Mrs. C. You totally do," agreed Jules.

"You're so sweet. Do you like my pearl earrings? A belated anniversary gift from your father," said Trudy just as Mr. Connors came into the room. He slipped his arm around Trudy's waist.

"We'd better get going if we're going to make our reservation," said Mr. Connors.

"Pull out the car, Paul. I'll be right there," said Trudy.

"Sure thing." He started to head out, then stopped and turned to Kat.

"Hey, Kitten. We still on for tennis in the morning?" he asked.

"You got it, Dad," Kat said, smiling. Mr. Connors winked at her and exited.

"Oh Kat, I forgot to tell you," said Trudy, getting her coat from the hall closet. "Zoe called this afternoon."

"Ugh! She's calling the house now? Tell her I've joined the circus."

"Kat, you've *got* to forgive her," Jules said. "The girl has no clue what to do with herself without you around to tell her. It's so pathetic. I mean, even *I'm* starting to feel sorry for her."

"Okay, but that doesn't mean I can't make her suffer a bit before I do."

"That goes without saying," said Jules. And both girls snickered.

"Well, I'll leave that drama for you girls to work out among yourselves. You kids be good tonight. We won't be back too late," said Trudy.

Mrs. Connors walked over to Kat and leaned over the sofa to give her a kiss. When she did, Kat whispered in her ear.

"I guess having that talk with Dad worked," said Kat.

"Yeah. And I have my very smart daughter to thank," said Trudy, giving Kat an extra tight hug. "She taught me what was really important."

Trudy grabbed her handbag and exited.

"Oh man! Kat! Check this out!" Kyle pointed to the TV and turned up the volume.

Kat, Jules, and Rory all looked and saw that a commercial for Glitter Girl had come on. It was loud and sparkly and featured the snotty Alpha Girl from Iowa parading around trying to look like all that. And she was wearing the engineer's cap!

Jules looked at Kat, a little worried. Not sure what Kat's reaction would be to seeing what she had given up in the name of their friendship. Kat stared at the screen for a long moment. Finally she spoke up.

"Okay. That is the stupidest hat ever!" she said.

Both Kat and Jules broke out in hysterical laughter. Kyle and Rory looked at each other, puzzled. They had no clue what the girls were laughing about. But then why would they?

After all, it was something that was only between best friends.

Acknowledgments

Writing a book might seem like a solitary endeavor, but in fact it could never happen without the support and guidance of others, and this novel is no exception. First, we would like to thank our agents and friends Tony Travostino and Carl Pritzkat, who first planted the idea of writing a book for young people in our heads and then tirelessly worked to find it a home once it had been completed. We also wish to thank our editor at Sourcebooks, Steve Geck, for his thoughtful read of our draft and insightful suggestions to improve the story. Also, we have to acknowledge the efforts of our attorney, Darren Trattner, whose good counsel and advice are always invaluable to legal Luddites like ourselves. And finally, we must thank our families, especially our spouses, Randy and Junko, for believing in us and allowing us to chase our dreams, regardless of how elusive they might seem. Your encouragement and love mean more to us than these meager words can convey.

About the Authors

Toni Runkle began her writing career at age four when she scrawled on a lampshade in crayon. Despite getting in *big* trouble, she continued writing (books, blogs, screenplays). She lives in Southern California with her husband and daughter, who are understandably grateful that she now writes on computers instead of furniture.

Stephen Webb hails from a small town in South Dakota and now lives in the small town of Los Angeles, where he enjoys annoying his wife and daughter by singing show tunes at the top of his lungs. He loves softball, cheeseburgers, and his family, although not necessarily in that order.